MENDING HEARTS

with the billionaire

Artists & Billionaires 6

MENDING HEARTS
with the billionaire

LORIN GRACE

CURRANT
CREEK PRESS

Cover Design © 2018 LJP Creative
Photos © iStock, Deposit Photos

Formatting by LJP Creative
Edits by Eschler Editing

Published by Currant Creek Press
North Logan, Utah

First edition: December 2018
ISBN: 978-1-970148-01-5

For Sally

DUMB LUCK CLUB FOREVER.

one

WISPY CLOUDS FLOATED PAST THE plane—or was the plane speeding past the clouds? Either way, they had Candace reminiscing.

Her footsteps echoing in the empty hallway, Candace slowed her step as she realized she didn't belong here anymore. Having made the choice to leave all that remained, she was to notify the dean of the College of Art. He had been patient long enough, as the answer had been due by the end of June. Now, two days late, she couldn't help but hope the dean had already left for the Independence Day break.

Light spilled from the office at the end of the hall. Her favorite professor was either in the building or had forgotten to lock up again. Candace peeked in as she passed. Dr. Christensen stood in front of an empty canvas, hands on hips. Delaying the inevitable, Candace knocked on the door.

"Come in, Candace. You're just in time to help me solve a dilemma. I'd planned on a blue underpainting, but the canvas keeps telling me sepia."

Candace took a piece of paper from the professor's desk and held it up to the canvas. "Your canvas isn't pure white."

"That is the problem. Thank you. Let me guess. You are here to officially tell the dean you won't be with us this fall."

1

"How did you know?"

Dr. Christensen pulled out a stool and indicated for Candace to sit. "You have been my student for eight years now. If you would ever turn in your signed forms, you would have a master of art in painting and another in art history, and I suspect enough extra credits and projects for a third in illustration. I've watched you teach freshman-level classes on and off for the last four years. You don't enjoy it. So even if you want the job, I'll protest."

Candace opened her mouth to protest, but Dr. Christensen held up his hand. "I am not sure what life holds for you around the next corner. That is the marvelous thing about corners—the not being able to see around them. Now, I have two suggestions for you: turn in the paperwork to get your double masters and turn that corner."

Studying the landscape below her, she wondered when Indiana became Ohio. For almost two months, she'd replayed the conversation in her mind. The problem was that she felt like the blonde from the old four-way stoplight joke. Gas, brake, gas, brake, unable to move forward as long as the light kept flashing. She couldn't even figure out which blinker to turn on. Yet somehow while she remained stuck, the world kept moving around her. Cruising at six hundred miles an hour at thirty thousand above the earth in Preston Harmon's private jet, it was more apparent than ever that everyone knew where they were going—except her.

A tiny wail took Candace's attention from the window to the seats behind her, where Mandy and Daniel sat with two-month-old Joy. It probably wasn't good to have a favorite roommate, but Mandy and Candace had felt an immediate connection that deepened with time and late nights over ice cream, where Candace had shared her deepest secrets.

But for her friend, life had moved on. Mandy had not only turned her corner when she married her childhood friend but had now entered a whole new world of diapers, blankets, and nursing-friendly tops. Out of habit, Candace stomped down the phantom desires before they led her down roads with dead-end signs. She watched as Daniel helped Mandy up and they moved to the privacy of the bedroom at the back of the plane so Mandy could feed Joy.

Example number two sat in front of her. Abbie Hastings Harmon craned her neck to track Mandy's progress to the back of the plane. Letting go of being Mandy's bodyguard wasn't easy for her, but Abbie had turned a corner too when she married Preston, finding new ways to use her talent at photography in her new husband's publishing empire. Candace suspected Abbie gave her own bodyguards fits and eventually had the best-trained security detail in the business. Becoming the one who was guarded hadn't stopped Abbie from being ultra-aware of her surroundings or having at least one gun concealed on her person. Preston whispered something in Abbie's ear that led to a kiss.

Candace returned her attention to the window. The reflection of her cousin Zoe studying a New York City guidebook reminded Candace that even Zoe was moving on. When Candace had decided not to accept the teaching job at the university, Zoe was still going to be her roommate for at least another semester. Her home, dubbed the Art House, wasn't going to be full, but she wouldn't be alone. Then, last week, Zoe had accepted a last-minute internship at the prestigious Scott & Ricks firm, leaving Candace roommate-less. The thought of having three empty bedrooms in Art House was almost as daunting as trying to fill them with students that seemed younger each semester.

Which brought her full circle to that corner where she needed to turn her life in a new direction.

Third wheel. Over the last year-and-a-half, a vague sense that he had become one filled Colin. The fact that third wheels could be extremely useful, such as in landing an airplane, helped him keep some balance. Traveling to a wedding with his best friend, who was now a father, intensified that feeling. He knew the bride as well as he knew any of Candace's roommates, and he'd met the groom a couple times. Unlike some of the women on the private flight, he didn't have to be a part of the wedding itself. He had debated about skipping it entirely, but two things had drawn him out of his computer-filled office—the opportunity to catch up with Nick Gooding, one of his few remaining single friends, and Candace.

She sat across the aisle from him. The private jet contained more than enough seats, so only the married couples and body-guards sat together. If he had been brave enough, he would have taken the seat next to her when they'd boarded.

Colin had read on some online blog that weddings made women think about more weddings, particularly their own. In the past year, Candace had been maid of honor at Mandy and Daniel's wedding, where he had been best man; a bridesmaid at Araceli and Kyle's wedding, which he hadn't attended; a brides-maid at Abbie's wedding, which he had participated in on very short notice; and on Friday she would be maid of honor at Tessa and Sean's Labor Day weekend wedding. So far she had caught the bouquet at every wedding. Although Abbie had just handed Candace hers as she'd run from the ballroom. He wasn't sure that counted. Statistically, Candace had to be thinking about marriage by now, even if she showed no outward signs.

If only he could get her to think of him when it came to mar-riage. Other than dancing, she had kept him literally at arm's length for all the 508 days of their acquaintance.

They had met online a year and a half ago, Daniel had been desperate to protect Mandy from the vipers unleashed by the paparazzi after their first date and had enlisted Colin's computer skills to set up firewalls and monitor threats. Even with Daniel's description of Mandy's unorthodox roommate, Colin had been unprepared for their first video conference. Daniel had only mentioned Candace's hair, not her eyes. Blue didn't do the color justice. Sometimes darker, sometimes lighter, that first day they were the deep blue of one of his favorite computer-brand logos. He suspected the shade changed with her mood, but he needed more research to be sure.

He took heart in the fact that she'd dumped or been dumped by a law student over a year ago and hadn't had another boyfriend since. And rarely did more than thirty-one hours and ten minutes go by without a text or video call with her. Although things hadn't been the same for the last couple months, Candace, who always had a plan and always knew her next gig, seemed like she was lost, and she wouldn't say why. Something had changed the day she got her last wig—the one to celebrate another year of being cancer free. He'd seen the change in her eyes. Mandy told him he was imagining things, but he wasn't. Colin was sure he wasn't imagining anything. For the past forty-two days, Candace's eyes had been a dull gray blue.

Gathering his courage, he moved to the leather seat facing her. "Penny for your thoughts."

She raised one of her painted brows. "Do you even have a penny?"

"I can transfer it via two or three different apps."

"But I don't need a penny."

"What do you need?"

"Chocolate?"

"I can do chocolate." He pulled up a shopping app. "It will be waiting at the Blue Pines Inn's front desk."

"Caramels and cherries?"

"Of course. And they are hand dipped in Blue Pines."

The first hint of a real smile flashed across her face.

"So how many of your thoughts does that get?"

Candace patted the seat next to her. "Probably not as much as it should. I was thinking about what Dr. Christensen told me about turning a corner. I just don't know where to go."

"What options do you have?"

"Far too many. But almost all of them mean I need to leave Art House. I have had so few commissions lately. Most of the jobs I've seen are murals. I just finished a children's book illustration project, but I'll be honest—the author drove me bonkers. She kept changing her mind. Part of my problem is I have not focused on one specialty. Now I have no roommates and no direction."

"Rethinking your choice not to continue at the school?"

"No. I even got my degrees in the mail the other day. They knew I wouldn't show up at the graduation."

"I don't understand why you would choose to skip graduation. Two master's degrees is something to celebrate."

Candace looked out the window before answering. "It was never in my plan to get a master's. I'm not sure what to do with one, let alone two of them."

"Plans can change."

"They aren't supposed to."

Colin studied his friend. "Mine change all the time. It is like this app I am working on to recognize doctored pictures. I'd planned on using a certain protocol, but when I got to testing it, I discovered it was inadequate for my needs. So I changed my plan."

"Not really. You are still making the app. Isn't that the one you are making because of the Abbie head-swap mess? The TV stations should have been able to tell that the photo had been manipulated to put her head on the woman wearing the negligee."

He waggled his finger at her. "No changing the subject. And yes, it is the app to help people identify faked online photos so they don't pass them along. But it isn't like I had this in my five-year plan or even my New Year's resolution. I didn't even have it planned four months ago because I didn't see the need. I had another app planned, but the newest version of a competitor's app does more than mine ever would, so I dumped it. See? Plans change."

"Yes, but your master plan hasn't changed. You are programming computers, leaving most of the business end of your life to Daniel and your lawyers."

"That is true. So, what isn't going according to your plan?"

"That's the problem. I don't have one anymore. I got to the end of my ten-year plan and was not where I assumed I would be."

"What about your twenty-year plan?"

"I didn't think I'd need one."

"Why not?"

Candace didn't answer. She twirled one of the green tendrils of her wig around her finger. She'd purchased the wig to celebrate another year of remission. Just as if he were looking at a bug in the middle of a long line of code, sudden understanding filled him.

"You didn't think you would live to see the end of your ten-year plan, did you?"

Candace shook her head and turned to retreat into the window view again. Colin didn't let her. He pulled her into a hug instead. She turned into his embrace. He held her, believing the words he wanted to say would not be well received.

I want to be part of your next ten-year plan.

two

THE SIX FORMER ROOMMATES SAT around a table in one of O'Malley's private rooms. Candace wondered how many times they would be gathering like this as their families and careers pulled them in different directions. Tessa had debated other locations for her party but decided on O'Malley's because it was the last place Sean would think she would go, as his outrageous Irish friend was just a little too brash and way too flirty. Tessa's description had fallen short of just how outrageous the pub owner was. All night he offered them free drinks in a fake Irish accent only to be turned down every time, as had his offers of kissing the bride and bridesmaids. His good-natured winks told them he was mostly teasing. Candace doubted he was as much of a flirt as he pretended to be.

Tessa opened Zoe's gift. "A blank book for a new life. You are still trying to get me to journal?"

"I believe in it, and what better time to start than when you are starting a new life with a new name?" Zoe's enthusiasm for journals was only eclipsed by their aunt's enthusiasm for genealogy—both passions Candace eschewed. Journals because she didn't wish her darkest hours on anyone and genealogy because, for the most part, it was boring. Although being a descendant of one of the first men to settle their Indiana county and who'd fought in the Revolutionary War was cool. Maybe she should plan a vacation to Massachusetts and see where the family once lived. If Zoe had a long weekend … Candace stopped the thought before it went too far. Neither she nor Zoe had a private plane or the resources most of her old roommates now had. She was getting very spoiled by association.

Tessa moved on to the other gifts. None of them were huge. After all, what did one get a woman who was marrying the country's newest billionaire? Candace never felt comfortable giving lingerie. Instead, she chose a painting of a field of bluebonnets at sunrise that Tessa had admired from the walls of Art House.

"Oh! Now I can always have a part of Art House with me!" Tessa drew her into a teary eyed hug.

As they had at every shower, the friends divided into two teams and created wedding dresses. This time they made them out of paper napkins rather than the traditional toilet paper since the party was at a restaurant. Mandy and Araceli joined Candace as they raced to make their dresses, the conversation quickly turning to Araceli's time in Haiti.

"I've reached the point that the children don't tease me about choosing the wrong Haitian-Creole word all of the time. Last month we took in several new children from a child-trafficking sting. They don't trust me because I am white, and they avoid Kyle. We are going to stay stateside for a couple months to help give them time to adjust and believe they are in a safe place. They don't trust white people." Araceli gathered one end of the napkins she held into a ruffle. "I'm looking forward to a few months in the States."

Mandy taped a sweetheart bodice together. "Your turn to be the model, Candace."

"I don't think so." She was never going to wear a wedding dress, paper or otherwise.

"We have both been models for the paper dresses. It is only fair you get a turn. Besides, if Joy decides she is hungry, it would ruin the dress." Mandy turned and checked on her sleeping daughter.

Araceli cut some napkins into ribbons. "She has a point, and I had to be the model at Mandy's party as well as my own, and y'all made the one quick dress at Abbie's half-hour long party before her wedding, which I wasn't invited to. I have never really had a chance to design."

Candace tried not to smile at Araceli's mixing of Texas lingo with her light Massachusetts accent. With three hours to prepare for Abbie's "real" wedding, flying in from Haiti hadn't been possible. Tessa hadn't been able to fly to Chicago from New York either. Since both Candace and Zoe were unlikely to marry soon, if at all, this could be the last hen party the roommates had. Arguing would kill the fun of the party, so Candace stood still as her friends worked feverishly to create a paper dress. Araceli worked on the sleeves. "Tell me all the news. Are you and Colin officially dating yet?"

Mandy tsked and shook her head. The other group stopped talking.

Candace answered louder than she needed to. "We are just friends. I am done with dating. I realize that with all the wedded bliss going on around here over the past year that this is hard for some of you to understand, but marriage is not for everyone. It's certainly not for me. Please stop asking about Colin. He. Is. A. Friend. I talk to him just like I talk to all of you."

"Really? You talk about everything? Even—" Tessa raised her brows.

"We don't discuss feminine hygiene if that is what you're asking. I don't think that is something he could handle hearing much about. And as I said, he is my friend, and sending him into a blushing fit is not one of my goals." Not like she'd told any of her female friends about the fact she didn't need to buy products as often lately. *My doctors believe I am already going into meno-*

pause—one of the side effects of having chemo at age sixteen. She hadn't had that conversation with anyone outside of the medical team. The big *M* word was for grandmothers, not women who hadn't reached their twenty-eighth birthday.

Not content to stick her foot in her mouth just once, Araceli turned her questions to Zoe. "So, are you going to follow the trend and find yourself a ten-figure husband? There should be one or two here in New York. Sean's other groomsman is single."

Glad to have the spotlight off her, Candace didn't attempt to stop the impending disaster.

Tessa joined in. "Nick Gooding is really nice, and he is one of the good guys. You should do something with us while you are living here."

"I don't think double dating with newlyweds would be that fun. Besides, as a graphic designer, I think I should be exempt from the curse. It is my duty to break it. So no thanks to the offer." Zoe broke off a piece of tape with her teeth.

"You never know. I am not really an artist at all." Abbie's wedding ring caught the light as she spoke. "I had no intention of falling in love on the job and not with one of those rich, snobby millionaire types I have worked with for years. Present company and their spouses excluded, of course."

"Daniel and Colin both went to school with Nick, and they like him. Just imagine how much fun we could have if you did marry him." Mandy added a tissue rose to the creation.

At Zoe's reddening face, Candace decided to end the torment. "I think it is about time for judging so we can clean up and be out of here. We only reserved the room until ten."

"I agree." Tessa tried to turn around in the dress taped around her body. "I don't really want to have O'Malley smirking at us for the next couple months for wearing paper goods."

Ten minutes later, Tessa declared the dresses a tie, and the paper creations were packed in a produce box for Tessa to use later. In less than twenty-four hours, another roommate would be walking down the aisle. Dreams Candace had packed away a decade ago—of orange blossoms, white satin, and lace—came back to haunt her.

Colin tried not to take his phone out of his pocket to see how well his latest app worked. He had never been one for large groups—not that the gathering of Sean's friends and the spouses of Tessa's friends was large, but he did feel out of place. He wasn't even an official boyfriend and had only been invited to the bachelor party, held in one of the private rooms at the Irish Pub owned by one of Sean's groomsmen, because of his association with Daniel Crawford and Nick Gooding. At least the party wasn't wild like those he had seen on TV. The classic video-game contest was something Colin could appreciate. He waited for another turn on the Pac-Man arcade game. The presence of Sean's grandfather, who was a minister, and the various bodyguards who worked for the men in the room may have been a factor in the low-key party.

Nick joined him in watching Preston Harmon fail at Frogger. "I wasn't expecting to see you here. How do you know Sean?"

"I don't. I think I was invited because Tessa thought Candace and I are dating and it evened out the numbers, since Sean's best man is married."

"But you came anyway?"

"I'd like to date Candace, and I was hoping another wedding might push her in that direction." If anything, the third wedding of the year was doing the opposite.

"Which one is Candace again?"

"The maid of honor. At the rehearsal, she was wearing the Van Gogh T-shirt." Most people described Candace by her wigs, which missed so much of who she was. Colin avoided the descriptor whenever possible.

"Zoe's cousin?" Nick mentioned the bridesmaid who was his partner for the ceremony.

"Yup. She—"

"Hey, Colin, beat that score!" Daniel shouted from the vintage Pac-Man game.

Colin nodded at Nick, happy to have the conversation over. Explaining why he was the odd man out wasn't improving his comfort level. If only women could be as logical as a video game.

Colin tried to forget all about women as he ran from the ghosts in the virtual maze. But the ghosts kind of looked like veiled brides, and he couldn't decide if he was the Pac-Man or if it was Candace running away from the idea. Great, now she was even on his mind when playing a game. The ghost tagged him, prompting the game-over screen. He watched as Sean earned one of the highest scores of the night. Not fair. If anything, it should be the groom who was distracted. He went on to play Frogger. Surely nothing could remind him of Candace in that game. Other than the way she teased him about the "fancy red car" he never drove. A purple race car squashed his frog.

Daniel shook his head as he took the controls. "Better luck next time."

Not a chance. Colin doubted he could win at any game unless he figured out the dating one first.

three

As the bride and groom waltzed around the marble floor of the restored Blue Pines courthouse-turned-museum, Candace wondered if they'd even noticed the rest of the people in the building. If dancing with your new husband was anything like dancing with Colin, then not only did the newlyweds not see the guests, they had entered their own little world.

Rats. She had only gone two minutes without thinking about him. She needed to put an end to the relationship before he got hurt. She hadn't intended for things to keep deepening between them. She met him near the end of year nine of her ten-year plan. At some point, she'd decided he would even be her tenth kiss, but she had never acted on the completion of that bucket-list item since the friendship had grown more intense than with any guy she had ever known. Colin had made her question all her teenage assumptions about men and drop that one item from her bucket list. Because of that, she had never even tried to kiss him, or anyone else, since she had gone out with the law student almost a year and a half ago.

Zoe sat down next to Candace as Tessa's mom and Sean's grandfather joined the dance. "We're up next."

"Speaking of which—how are you getting along with Nick?"

"We'll survive the day." Zoe had barely finished the sentence when Nick and the best man joined them.

Candace loved dancing. However, the best man had barely mastered the two-step shuffle. It was a relief when Colin cut in and they could do their own variation of the fox-trot. It had been a pleasant surprise last year at Mandy and Daniel's wedding, where she had also been the maid of honor, to learn that Colin danced—and not just the standard moves. He danced ballroom, including the cha-cha and tango, and he led with the finesse of Fred Astaire.

"Do you think you can swing in that dress?" Colin spun her out.

"East Coast or West?"

"Texas push."

Candace took an extra step. "Maybe, but nothing fancy. The skirt is too long for any flips."

The current song ended. The tempo of the next song was faster. "Did you manage to sneak a salsa beat into their playlist?"

"Maybe." Candace started the basic step, encouraging Colin.

"You know I need to work on this one."

"One, two, three, five, six, seven." She counted out the beats, skipping four and eight, where the dancer's feet remained in place.

Colin laughed. "Not that much help. Just practice. You should come to Chicago, and we could find a place to dance."

His neck reddened as it had more often of late. Candace wasn't sure how to answer. He had been hinting about a date for months, never getting closer than a vague "maybe we could."

"There is a new studio opening this weekend. Come up next week, and we can try it out." Colin maneuvered a turn.

Candace spun away from him, not sure how to answer. "I hate crashing at Mandy's. Maybe some other time."

"Why crash at the Crawford's? You can use the VIP apartment Abbie lived in."

So much for that excuse. "That apartment has eyes in the walls."

The security features had been enhanced during Abbie's stay, giving new meaning to Big Brother as all four of Abbie's brothers had taken their turn monitoring their sister's undercover activities.

"Hastings security removed all of their equipment when Abbie got married. It is back to normal. Just the security pad on the door and standard alarm system. No cameras, no microphones."

The song ended.

"I'll check my calendar. Would you mind getting me some water?" Candace sat down at a table, hoping to come up with a way out of going to Chicago. Dancing, yes. Dating, no.

Colin met Nick on a similar errand.

"Ogilvie, I had no idea you could dance like that. Next time I get one of those invitations to be on *Dancing with Divas*, I'll refer them to you."

National television. There could not be a worse nightmare. "Please, no. I only can dance with Candace."

"Is everything all right?"

This was not the place to explain. "Just tired of the friend zone."

"Candace?" asked Nick.

Colin accepted two water glasses from the wait staff. "Who else? I was hoping now that she will be roommate-less I could get her to come to Chicago more, but she is more averse to change than anyone I have ever met."

"I thought Zoe lived with her. Wait—she is the one with the internship, right? Doesn't Candace have other roommates?"

"Candace hasn't been replacing her roommates these past few months."

The waiter handed Nick the lemon water he'd requested. Nick took a napkin as well.

Colin ventured a question to change the subject. "What's up with you and Zoe? Watching you laugh in the carriage on the way over, I thought you had a connection with her, but she has pulled one of her disappearing acts."

"You were watching us?"

"Candace was. It looked more than friendly to me." *Surprising* was a better word, but he could be wrong.

"I am not sure we are even at friendly. She is keeping to herself."

"She is a Wilson woman. Runs in the family. Good luck." Colin raised one of the water glasses before walking in the direction of the tables.

Not sure whether to be buoyed up or downhearted in discovering that Nick also had difficulties with women, Colin took the long way around the room back to Candace. Perhaps he should ask her on a date outright, but it was not anything he had ever done before. Where was one to seek such advice? For the last six months, his usual mode of learning had failed him. The advice he found online was either aimed toward seduction or sounded as if it came out of a cheap romance novel. Unlike programing, there were no reliable message boards with expert advice. Using multiple search engines and query strings hadn't helped.

How had Daniel, Kyle, Preston, and Sean all managed to get the women they loved to marry them? And in less than six months? There must be some formula he was missing. After all, some of the singles sites claimed to match couples based on algorithms, so there must be a formula for falling in love too.

When he wasn't dancing, he spent the rest of the reception studying various couples, trying to figure out what elusive concept he'd missed.

After the bouquet and garter toss, he danced the last few dances with Candace, who managed to duck catching the bouquet entirely. As they waltzed along the edge of the floor in the shadows of the room, every once in a while, Colin would notice a couple other than the bride and groom kissing on the dance floor or wandering out of the main gallery. What would Candace do if he tried to kiss her? It hadn't been the first time he had wondered about the effects of a kiss on their relationship. Frankly, it was impossible to dance the tango with this woman and not wonder. Not that he ever dared find out.

Colin worked to steer Candace toward a column that partially blocked the view of the north alcove from the dance floor. When he was only three yards away, the song ended, and someone took the mike and announced it was time to see the bride and groom off.

"That is me." Candace gathered her skirts and nodded before crossing the floor.

Colin looked longingly at the column. The entirety of their relationship could be summed in the remaining nine feet. So close...

Guests filtered out of the museum after the departure of the bride and groom. The bridesmaids left in the limo headed back to the Blue Pines Inn. Candace and Zoe offered Colin a seat, but he had no desire to be caught in the middle of a bunch of giggling girls.

Nick joined him. "Are you staying at the inn?"

"I didn't want to stay in the city." There were not any other options in the tiny town of Blue Pines.

"Come out to the family house with me. There is plenty of room, and the remainder of the wedding party isn't on the floor above you."

"That sounds like a deal I can't pass up." The women weren't bad, but they tended to talk too much, and being the only single guy was as awkward as the time he'd impulsively corrected his advanced calculus teacher in front of the class.

Nick pulled out his keys. "My car is around back. Let's get your things."

The short drive from the museum to the edge of Blue Pines passed in a blur. Nick barely slowed down as the gate at the end of his drive rolled back to let them enter.

Colin gave a low whistle as Nick rounded the curve of the drive and the nineteenth-century mansion came into view. "My mother would kill for a place like this. She is forever complaining our place is too modern for her."

"Welcome to the Cottage." Nick indicated that Colin should leave his suitcase with the butler who greeted them. "He'll get that up to your room. Do you want the grand tour or the shortest way to my man cave?"

A yawn proceeded Colin's answer. "I think the man cave sounds good for now."

"So, how long have you been dating Candace?"

"You mean how long have I been *trying* to date Candace? That woman has more tricks for keeping a relationship in the friend zone than the Pentagon has to keep hackers out. The Pentagon is easier to hack."

Nick gave Colin a sideways glance. "I am not sure I want to know about that."

"I was only twelve. Thanks to Dad's money, they didn't make a big deal of the break-in other than making me create a fix for the hack I exposed. Why are women so difficult?"

"I have no idea." Nick shook his head. He turned the conversation back to Colin. "How long have you been interested in Candace?"

"Since I first saw her spiky pink hair on my computer screen over a year ago. 512 days."

Nick whistled and shook his head. "And she won't date you?"

"Nope, I tried for a kiss last New Year's Eve and came up all cheek. The annoying thing is I know about all these guys she has kissed. Not that she has since some law student activist dumped her to go protest in California. She tries to keep me in the friend zone by talking about the guys she's dated like I am one of the Art House women. But the guys she kissed don't know her at all. She doesn't let them see anything beyond her rotating wig collection before she moves on."

"That explains a lot. I thought I saw her the other day down on the square, but since her hair was different, I thought I was mistaken."

"My favorite wig she has is this blonde, with green ends. Ombre or something, but it's soft and sassy just like her."

"Oh, you have it bad. What are you going to do?"

"I need a new idea. Maybe you can help." Colin took a breath and dove in. "Nothing is keeping her in Indiana. If I could find a way to get her to come to Chicago, maybe we could spend more time together. When she does come up, we are always with Mandy and Daniel. If she lived there, we could spend more one-on-one time together. From the articles I have read, that is important."

"You read articles about dating?"

Colin hated the fact that his face heated up. "While you and Daniel were flirting with girls, I was programming. I may have missed out on some social milestones."

Nick kept a straight face.

Colin defended himself. "They wouldn't write the articles unless there were other guys like me who needed them."

"Maybe they are for you. After all, you were the only one without a photo in *Forbes* last year, and the word most linked with you is *reclusive*." This time Nick did laugh.

"On the bright side, I can walk down the street without a bodyguard, especially if I wear my contacts. I don't think there is a single photo out there of me without a pair of thick glasses."

"That's what is different. I don't think I have seen you without your glasses often."

"One of the articles said that nerds needed to go for the contacts and improve their image."

Nick squinted at him. "I don't think Candace is one of those women who judges much by the cover."

"I know, but 512 days." Colin looked at his watch. "Make that 513. I need something to change." The poor squished game frog had a better chance at crossing the road than he did.

"What does Candace do?"

"She is an amazing artist."

"Probably can't try the old hire-her-as-your-secretary routine, then."

"I've thought of hiring her to do a mural in one of my buildings, but she would say it was a pity job. She hasn't had too many commissions lately." There was one building that did need a mural, but it was in South Bend, Indiana, closer to Art House than to him.

"I think I have an idea. A couple of years ago I purchased a two-story turn-of-the-century carousel. My thought was to fix it up and donate it to, well … that doesn't matter, but I still have the carousel packed away in a warehouse. It needs a lot of work. If it had the right artist …"

"I have a new warehouse—nice and clean, state-of-the-art ventilation. It's never been used and is just the place to undertake the major refurbishment of an antique."

"Now if you only knew an artist. Maybe one with spiky pink hair. Then I would be happy to send the carousel out to Chicago and hire her."

Colin grinned. That might just work. "Nick Do-Gooder Gooding, you are a genius!"

"Now, do you have any ideas about how to break the ice with her cousin?"

"Sorry, but if I come up with anything, I'll let you know." Colin yawned. "Do you mind pointing me in the direction of my room?"

The bedroom had enough plugs for all his devices, including USB plugs—not what he expected in an older building. Colin turned Nick's idea over in his mind. He could offer to put Candace up in one of his apartment buildings, specifically his. Then they could easily spend more real time, not screen time, talking, and then … As Colin worked through potential scenarios, the emotional fatigue of keeping his feelings bottled up and from the events of the day kicked in. Even his computers and apps weren't enough to keep him going. Day 513 ended like it had started, thinking of Candace. He had read that was how you knew you were in love—when you fall asleep and wake up thinking about one person.

four

LATE SATURDAY MORNING, CANDACE WAS helping Zoe find some furniture to rent for Sean's old apartment, which only had a broken-down couch and scarred kitchen table. Araceli had caught a plane back to Haiti. Preston and Daniel had both texted their wives and taken Abbie and Mandy to various places. After purchasing a new bed to be delivered this afternoon, Zoe only needed a couple more items.

Candace ran her hand over a bookcase in the next store. "I still can't believe everyone is moving on so fast. I didn't see Abbie ever getting married. I thought she was a safe roommate."

"I'll be back." Zoe turned over a price tag.

"I bet you a semester's rent Scott & Ricks hires you as soon as you get your diploma in December. You won't be back." Everyone was moving on, letting their lives ebb and flow, but Candace felt as if hers was stuck behind a giant dam and she had nowhere to go. But then again, the corner Dr. C had talked about required a choice.

Zoe's face lit up. "Wouldn't that be wonderful? Scott & Ricks is the kind of place every freshman hopes to work when they graduate. But this place is not Indiana. I am not naive enough to think living in the city will be easy. I am such a country mouse."

"The old song says, if you can make it here you can make it anywhere." Candace sat in a chair and wished she could buy it for her own place. "Oh, try this one."

Zoe tried the upholstered recliner. "What are you going to do since you turned down the teaching job?"

"I have some commissions lined up, though not as many as I would like. But I have enough work for now." It was a lie. She had a book cover and some Valentine's day illustrations for a card company.

"Have you considered selling Art House?"

"Why? Where would I go? I have an amazing studio space and everything I need." Everything but friends. When had the freshmen gotten so young? She had taught half the grad students and hadn't really connected with them. If she kept getting room-mates from the local college, it wouldn't be long before she felt like some dorm mom.

"Including two empty bedrooms? Three, if you count mine." Zoe raised her brow. "I think I'll take this chair."

"Mandy comes down regularly."

"Do you think she will close up her little house now that they have a mansion under construction closer to Chicago? She already travels less because of Joy." Zoe wrote down the ID number of the chair on an order form.

Candace didn't answer. Married friends were great, but they were married, and no matter how much they said it didn't change things, it did. No more 2:00 a.m. chats over ice cream and only half the secrets because husbands became best friends.

Zoe interrupted her thoughts. "You had your ten-year plan and bucket list. Check, check and double check. It's time for a new plan. You know as well as the rest of us that Colin wants more than friendship."

Her cousin knew more about Candace's plans and condition than anyone. Why couldn't Zoe understand that more than friendship just wasn't possible? "No. I can't. You and I may have different reasons for remaining single, but mine are just as valid."

"A decade has shown your reasons may be wrong." Zoe opened a dresser drawer.

"Just because I am here having this discussion with you doesn't mean my reasons have changed. And what about yours? Not every man in the world is a selfish jerk. Perhaps your reasons need to change too." Candace knew it was low to change the point of the conversation, but she wasn't the only one who needed to move on. Zoe needed a push more than she did.

Zoe glared. "My reasons are never going to change."

"Mine can't." A tear formed near the corner of Candace's eye. No way was she going to cry here. That was reserved for the privacy of her own room.

"You don't know that, things are already different." Zoe crossed her arms just like she did when she was three.

Candace rushed out of the store before the tears could come and hailed the first cab she saw. Only after the driver asked her a destination did she realize she had no idea where she was going.

Colin hadn't planned on leaving until Sunday, but after nailing down some plans with Nick, he decided to return to Chicago early. Having booked a first-class seat to the Windy City, Colin found himself on the two o'clock flight. He took advantage of the plane's Wi-Fi to catch up on neglected emails. Candace's IM popped up.

—What are you doing this evening? Still at Nick's?

No, I caught a flight back to Chicago.

—I thought you were going with us tomorrow.

Something important came up.

One article advised that he should make himself less available if he wanted to move out of the friend zone. That hadn't been his entire reason for leaving early, but it had played a part. There had been no definite plans for the evening, and he didn't want to be a backup plan if Candace got bored.

—**K. Have a good flight.**

Thanks, see you later.

Part of him wanted to chat more. But that would be making himself available. And she was with her cousin and friends, so it wasn't like she needed him.

Candace never needed him. Not really. She had too many friends. Maybe if she lived in his building she would at least need him as a neighbor—borrow a cup of sugar or something. Did he even have sugar?

Colin had no idea what most of the cupboards in his penthouse held. His housekeeper, Janie, made meals and froze them so he could eat whenever he wanted. If he didn't go through them fast enough, she would give him a piece of her mind, telling him that man couldn't live off electricity and that he needed to get out of his brain more. Only when he claimed to have been on a date did she soften her approach. Janie had worked for his parents for years before taking the job with him. He speculated his mother was paying Janie a bonus to spy on him. Considering that working for him full-time probably amounted to less than fifteen hours a week, Janie probably made more per hour than the city's top executives. She deserved it. He wouldn't trust anyone else not to interfere with the projects that lay strewn throughout the place.

Candace probably wouldn't want to borrow sugar anyway. More likely he should keep ice cream in the freezer. Or not. Then he could take her out.

He turned his attention back to his computer, studying the variables in the line of code. It was one problem he knew he could solve by the time they landed. Then his afternoon would be clear to prepare for project Merry-Go-Round.

five

At Grand Central Station, Candace only had to wait twenty minutes for the next train out to Blue Pines. She had planned to spend the evening with Zoe and have Abbie and Preston pick her up after the Broadway show they were attending. For a moment, she debated taking another cab to Zoe's place, but they both needed the space. Unfortunately, Colin wasn't around either, meaning she would probably spend the evening alone in a city she didn't know.

The Saturday afternoon train was mostly empty, so she didn't have to share a seat. The quiet gave her time to think. Other than the conductor's voice, which was smooth in a chocolate-fondue sort of way, no one interrupted her. She tried to concentrate on the river and buildings framed by her window, but she couldn't get past the essence of their fight. What if her younger cousin was right? Could marriage be an option, or had all of the flowers fogged her brain?

She was the only passenger to disembark at Blue Pines. Rather than go to the inn, Candace walked in the direction of the old church, now a community center, where yesterday's wedding was held. Across the street was a city park complete with bandstand and small gazebo. No wonder Hearthfire had chosen to film one of their famous Christmas movies here. Candace wandered past the playground and watched parents push their children on the swings. A father waited at the bottom of a slide as his daughter sat on the top, refusing to go down. An older child in a matching shirt gave the reluctant child a shove. Giggles filled the air.

Candace turned away. She'd once had dreams of taking her own children to the park. She'd also had dreams of joining one of America's premier ballet companies. But that had all changed with one little lump. Everything had changed.

A familiar figure sat alone in the little gazebo.

"Hello, Reverend Cavanagh," she greeted Sean's grandfather.

He waved her over to the bench beside him. "Candace, right? I love your blue hair. However, do young people change styles so fast?"

In answer, she lifted the wig a couple inches to reveal her bald head.

"Did you shave it?"

"No. I managed to acquire the rare condition of chemotherapy-induced alopecia. Unlike other cancer patients, when my therapy was done, my hair didn't come back."

The reverend nodded. "I am glad to see you make the most of your condition. I have often wondered what I would have looked like with different hair. As a child, it was bright red. Now nice people call it silver. I once wondered if I would have been luckier with the girls if my hair wasn't so fiery."

"Tessa said you had been married fifty years. I think you got pretty lucky, even with red hair."

"My wife was a wonderful woman, and I was lucky to have her. What about you? Have you found that lucky one yet?"

Candace bit her lip. Something about the old minister invited her to bare her soul. Maybe it would help to talk. It wasn't like she was likely to see him again, and didn't he have to keep everything confidential? "I've never looked because I can't get married."

"Why not?"

Candace pulled the battered 4 x 6 notebook from her purse. "Because I am supposed to be dead. The first time I was in the hospital, I heard the doctor talking out in the hall. He said he only gave me ten years. So I made a ten-year plan and a bucket list." She handed the reverend the notebook. "I've done almost everything I set out to do. I spent a night in the Cinderella Castle and even got to wear one of the costumes. I've been kissed at the top of the Empire State Building, although I have no clue what his name was—one of my mistakes. I graduated and made a difference in my school by making it popular not to drink. And I modified some of my list as I discovered that some things were not as important as others. Like eating chocolate ice cream over going vegan. There is nothing left to do."

Reverend Cavanagh held up the last page. "Except this?"

She didn't need to look at the page he held. The sketch of a headstone, one of her first, was poorly executed. "Except that. Believe me, I have no intention of making that happen. I just thought after all these years that it would happen, but it hasn't. I should have died last year, and now I don't know what to do."

"The same as the rest of us. You keep living. Doctors make guesses. Sometimes they are wrong. Maybe that doctor wasn't even talking about you. You said you overheard the doctor, so there is a chance, isn't there?" He handed her notebook back.

Candace put it in her purse. "I guess he could have been talking about someone or something else. But—"

"It may not surprise you, but I believe in prayer and miracles. Do you pray?" There was a twinkle in his eye that made it almost impossible not to believe in God.

"Yes, I believe in prayer. I know it got me through my treatment. Sometimes the answers are not what we want. Near the end of her life, my mother asked us to stop praying she would live." Praying Mom would die had been the most challenging prayer she'd ever uttered. The fact that it had been answered only hours later gave her as much peace as it did anger.

"You lost your mother?"

"She died of cancer. We went through some of our treatments together, though hers was more advanced than mine." Candace pretended to study the tall pine trees in the center of the park as the threat of tears passed.

The reverend gave her several minutes before he spoke again. "What do your doctors say about your condition now?"

"Given that I have been cancer free for nine years, they say I am likely to die of old age."

"Then I would consider that a miracle."

"But what if I die in ten years? It isn't fair to leave a husband and children." *If* she could even conceive.

"My son was a firefighter. Loved the job, his wife, and Sean. He had no idea when he went to work on September 11 that he would never come home again. But I don't think he spent time worrying about the what-ifs. He saved many lives that day and in the dozen or so years before. Even knowing that his job was riskier than most didn't stop him from enjoying life and his son. None of us has a guarantee."

Candace pondered that. Was she looking for a guarantee?

Reverend Cavanagh waited until her eyes met his. "Have you prayed about what to do?"

She shook her head.

"Maybe you should." The reverend's phone pinged. "That's my daughter-in-law wondering where I am. I'll add you to my prayers." He got up, smiled at Candace, and headed in the direction of the old church.

As the shadows in the park lengthened, Candace meandered back to the inn, contemplating Reverend Cavanagh's words. Could she make another ten-year plan? The thought both scared and excited her. A new bucket list? This time, instead of putting down that she wanted to kiss ten guys, she would choose only one, and she would have to love him. What did that even feel like? After blocking it out as an option for so long, Candace realized she wasn't sure. Maybe it was an illusion, like a Hearthfire movie.

Colin had the driver go straight to the warehouse from O'Hare. He'd built it last year mostly to test some ideas about solar energy and automation. The lighting would need to be improved, and perhaps a couple of rooms divided off. Restoration work probably involved sanding and chemicals to clean and refurbish the old wood. Candace would need a clean area to paint in that didn't have sawdust or smell of chemicals. She preferred natural light, but that wasn't feasible in this building. Artificial would have to do. Colin jotted down a few notes and emailed his contractor, knowing the man wouldn't be able to start until after Labor Day.

Colin took a couple pictures of the space and texted them to Nick. He didn't expect an answer right away and was surprised when one came.

—**Space looks good. May need a few divisions for different types of work. Let me know when you can get a contractor in.**

I will.

—**Good luck with operation Merry-Go-Round.**

The rest of the weekend was quieter than usual. The only real surprise was the contractor getting back to him Monday morning and indicating that changing the configuration of the warehouse would take less than ten days once the plans were drawn up and approved. Colin sent the notes over to the architect who had helped plan the building. Despite Monday being a holiday, plans and permits were approved and secured by noon on Tuesday.

Colin thought he was doing an excellent job of balancing his normal activities and overseeing the warehouse transformation until Daniel called him on it Thursday morning.

"I thought as the new dad I was the one supposed to resemble a zombie. What's up?" Daniel sat in his usual chair for their weekly meeting.

Not knowing how much his business partner would tell his wife, Colin answered carefully. "I'm collaborating with Nick on a personal project, and I guess I got too obsessive on my end."

Daniel studied Colin for an uncomfortable minute. "Nick mostly does real estate, not tech. What could you be partnering on?"

"It is one of his Do-Gooding things. He needed a state-of-the-art space to renovate an antique merry-go-round, and I have the one I built as a test project. It's more of a collaboration."

"And nothing else? A warehouse doesn't explain why you left New York early or moved the app to testing."

Hiding the truth from Daniel was as impossible as keeping the specs on his latest tech from his competitors the week before launch. Colin rubbed his forehead. "I'll tell you, but you have to promise not one word outside of this room, especially to your wife."

Daniel raised a brow. "You know there isn't much I would keep from her."

"She can't know."

"Fine. Our secret—unless it is illegal."

"Not illegal. Nick is going to hire Candace to work on the restoration of this old merry-go-round so she will move up to Chicago."

"And why would this be a secret? Won't Candace know she is being hired?"

"Nick is doing it for me. I want to spend more time with Candace." His face heated.

A smile filled Daniel's face. "It's about time. You have our support."

"You can't tell Mandy. If Candace realizes we made up the entire job just so she would move here...well, you know how she can get." Colin thought of the protest against Daniel selling his grandfather's mansion Candace had spearheaded. Her passion for correcting wrongs was one of the things he adored about her.

The most significant risk of project Merry-Go-Round was that she would see through the con and end it.

"I won't tell Mandy, but I may suggest a double date or two. We could even have to back out at the last minute if it would help." Daniel's idea had some merit. A couple double dates might help. "However, this not telling Mandy goes two ways. I won't break any confidences she shares with me about Candace."

"I wouldn't expect you to. Now, how do you think the new trade deal will affect our interests in Canada?" Colin ignored Daniel's knowing grin at the change of subject.

six

CANDACE DIDN'T RECOGNIZE THE NEW York number. Assuming the call was either Tessa or Zoe calling about the 9/11 ceremony, she answered. The deep voice on the other end was unfamiliar.

"Candace Wilson? This is Nick Gooding. Do you have a few minutes?"

If she didn't, she would have made time just out of curiosity. "I have time. I'm between projects." Days in between, but he didn't need to know that.

"Colin gave me your number. I have a project, and I understand you might be the artist I need."

More curious. "What type of project?"

"A couple years ago I purchased an old carousel with the idea of fixing it up and donating it to a park for children with special needs. However, the project fell apart, and I want to do something with it, although I am not yet sure what that will be. I am afraid it isn't good for it to just sit in storage, so now is the time to move forward. I've had a couple of restoration specialists repairing the mechanisms and broken animals, but the big problem is the painting."

"I've never done restoration work."

"I showed Tessa some of the photos. There is a mural on the central tower and operating station, actually two—one upper and one lower."

"Just a minute. Two levels?" She'd only ever seen one such carousel, and that had been in Portugal.

"A rather rare find. Some of the carousel animals and benches have intricate paintings and designs."

Candace tried to imagine what the carousel looked like. "I'm intrigued."

"I can send you the photos I have. The last photos were taken before World War II."

"Will I need to come to New York?"

"No, the carousel is currently at a warehouse in Chicago. I understand you need air returns and filters better than OSHA requires. The facility has what you need. If something is lacking, I'll be happy to pay for any upgrades."

He'd done his homework. Candace couldn't help but wonder if he'd had a bit of help with the idea. Her list of conspirators was long. Half her roommates could be behind the unexpected offer. "I don't even know how to bid on such a project."

"I expect it will take nearly a year to complete, so how about $100,000 plus housing near Mandy and Daniel?"

Thank goodness she wasn't on a video call. She was sure her mouth was hanging open. "That is more than generous."

"You don't need to answer tonight. Take a trip up to Chicago and look over the carousel. Also, if you feel you need to hire some extra hands, I have a budget for that."

"I'll drive up in the morning." She hoped she didn't sound too eager.

"I was told you might." Nick chuckled on the other end of the call. "I'll email you when I have the keypad code to the warehouse."

"Thanks. I'll let you know if I'm going to take the job after I see the carousel tomorrow."

"Thanks, Candace. I'll talk to you tomorrow."

He probably assumed she would take the job, and he would be right. Unless she felt it was beyond her skills.

Candace powered up her laptop and started searching for anything that might help her figure out what types of paints restoring an antique carousel might require.

She opened her IM program and messaged Colin.

I'm coming up to Chicago tomorrow to look at a merry-go-round. Do you know anything about that?

It was about three minutes before there was an answer.

—Would that be the one Nick has in one of my warehouses?

In your warehouse?

—A state-of-the-art one that Nick thought would work for this project he has. I knew he needed an artist. I assume he contacted you.

Only if I get to assume you recommended me for the job.

—It may have come up that I happened to know an excellent artist who was looking for a job.

Candace was torn between being thankful and wanting to turn down the job if Colin had gone behind her back to secure it. Desperation outweighed caution. Perhaps this was the corner she'd been searching for. The antique carousel was too tempting. She'd never have another opportunity like this. And maybe she could convince Nick to donate it to a location that would benefit children with cancer.

Let me guess. The apartment Nick offered is in one of your buildings.

—I think the one Abbie used while she was undercover is still available. The Hastings removed all the extra cameras.

That's in your building, isn't it?

—Only ten floors below my penthouse. Are you going to be my neighbor?

Maybe.

—See you tomorrow?

Do you want me to drop by the office or something else?

—How about dinner? We can celebrate your new job.

You're that sure I'll take it?

—Sure enough I've had the apartment cleaned and redecorated.

Candace laughed. She might be roommate-less, but at least she wasn't friendless.

So is it ready for me to move in?

—As soon as you want to.

I assume you don't want me painting the walls.

—I think you'll be busy enough with the horses. But if not, feel free to.

See you tomorrow.

Candace closed up the computer, then packed enough for a couple days. If she was going to close the house for a year, there were a lot of things she needed to come back and take care of on the weekend.

Dinner? Where? He couldn't just get takeout and eat in the office like they had before. There was that restaurant where Preston proposed to Abbie, but it was a little over the top for this date.

"Sabrina, top five restaurants in Chicago for first dates."

A computerized voice answered with a list of restaurants that served dates in puddings, pies, salads…

Colin rubbed his forehead and groaned. His household AI was not nearly as intelligent as it was artificial. "Sabrina, list of top ten restaurants in Chicago."

"Italian or Chinese?" the female voice asked.

Knowing the AI would just continue asking questions, Colin pulled out his phone and typed in his request. Within seconds, he had a list of possibilities. He chose one of the midrange restaurants, so not too fancy or over-the-top but something that didn't shout chain food.

A quick glance at the online menu showed they didn't serve any weird items.

Colin wondered if he should order flowers. "Sabrina, order a bouquet of flowers. Card to read "Congratulations on your new job" to be delivered to this building at 4:00 p.m."

"What is my budget?"

He had no idea. He tried to picture the flower shop he walked past occasionally. They often had signs in the windows. "$100."

"Okay. I have ordered one bouquet to be delivered at 4:00 p.m. Card reads 'Congratulations.'"

"Sabrina find me something to watch on TV."

A rerun of an eighties comedy started playing. At least part of her intelligence protocols worked. Colin sat on the couch and ran some tests on his latest app. Halfway through the show, the channel changed and a Hearthfire movie came on.

"Sabrina, why did you change the channel?" Colin glared at the little yellow pyramid that housed her microphone.

"This is a romance based on the troupe 'friends to lovers.' It is on your list of research topics. Watch it. You might learn." The computerized voice's inflection reflected her sarcasm. It was a bad idea to attempt to program personality.

"Sabrina, remind me to change your humanization coding around line 870."

"When should I remind you?"

"Sabrina, after the movie is over. And, Sabrina, do not change the channel."

The movie actually looked promising. The couple shared an interest in computer games. Colin studied the actors, wondering if he'd learned enough to accurately guess when the couple would share their first kiss—a moment in his own life he felt utterly unprepared for.

The movie ended with the couple kissing after a proposal. Sadly, Colin didn't feel as if he'd learned what he wanted to. Real people couldn't be as stupid as these characters were. The protagonist had nearly married the wrong guy just because he'd worn a suit. Suits were overrated. He'd take a T-shirt any day. Or a button-up flannel in the winter. The kiss hadn't taught him anything. The camera zoomed in to catch the triangle path of the guy's eyes around her face before he touched his lips to hers. She gave a foot pop, something he suspected was all Hollywood.

"Time to change the programming on line 870."

Colin reached for his laptop. "Sabrina, please power off."

Three beeps answered him as the AI unit shut down. Colin opened her control program and worked on giving his virtual helper an attitude adjustment. He also adjusted her search-engine feature—although it could be a glitch about what the AI knew about him. Dates with a woman weren't precisely in the history he had taught Sabrina. But with any luck, the AI would learn all about them very soon.

seven

MOST OF THE CAROUSEL PIECES remained packed in original wooden crates from the 1940s. In one of the rooms, three people were at work cleaning and restoring an exquisitely carved lion. The female employee nodded at her when she waved, though no one spoke. But then it may have been difficult through the filter masks they wore.

There was a room set up for her to paint in. The artificial light there mimicked natural light better than anything she had ever seen. Colin must have ordered the fixtures especially for her. Nick wouldn't have known her preferences. She turned on the air-filtration system, and a low hum filled the room. The user manual lay on one of the work tables. It was state-of-the-art hospital-grade filtration that would keep any dust out. Nick had made it very hard to turn down this job—or Colin had.

As she left the warehouse, Candace dialed Nick's number and got voicemail. "Hi, it's Candace. I am at the warehouse. Probably not a surprise, but I'll take the job. Bye." She hated leaving messages, but texting her new employer seemed too informal.

The early afternoon traffic wasn't bad, but the congestion of the city would be the worst part of the job. The underground-parking attendant at the apartment building handed her a pass.

"Parking space C11. Stop at the security. They have your keys. Have a good evening, Ms. Wilson." Apparently Colin had been very sure she would take the job.

She pulled the large suitcase from her trunk and wished she had packed more than a couple days' worth of clothing.

A humongous arrangement of flowers, the type sent to funeral homes, stood next to the security desk. Lavender-and-white gladiolas, mums, and lilies flowed gracefully from the vase. The family of a recently deceased resident must have donated them to the guards.

"Excuse me. I was told I could pick up my keys here?"

A uniformed guard or doorman—Candace wasn't sure if there was a distinction as she didn't see a weapon—double-checked his monitor. "Ms. Wilson? May I see your ID?" Again, he must have been expecting her as he knew her name.

Candace handed over her driver's license. He barely looked at it before handing it back with an electronic key. "I just need you to sign here." He handed her a tablet she signed with her finger.

The guard took the tablet back. "These flowers are for you. Should I have someone deliver them to your apartment?"

"For me?"

The guard handed her a florist's card.

Candace opened it.

Congratulations. Colin.

The impersonal computer type lent no warmth to the generic message and funeral display.

Candace started laughing the kind of laugh that usually came at 2:00 a.m. after a week of finals. The kind that didn't stop easily and brought tears to your eyes. Only Colin could manage to send congratulatory funeral flowers. She caught her breath. "Yes, if you could have someone bring them up." She tried not to laugh all the way to the elevator. Once inside and alone, she let the laughter bubble out. She started to text the group and realized she had forgotten to take a photo. The text would have to wait.

The apartment looked different than when Abbie had lived there. The ultramodern furniture in the living room had been replaced with softer, more traditional pieces. The bed was made up with only a set of sheets. A gift card to a bed-and-bath store lay were the pillow should be, along with a note.

Extra blankets in the closet. Get something you like. C

The buzzer rang. Candace opened the door, the flower arrangement half obscuring the uniformed delivery man. He set the monstrosity just far enough inside that he could close the door behind him as he left. She tried to move it into the living room and nearly toppled it, sending her into another fit of laughter.

As she collapsed into the comfy chair, her phone rang and Nick's number flashed on the screen. Candace took several deep breaths before swiping the answer button.

"Hello?" She heard the laughter in her own voice.

"Candace, are you okay?"

She took a deep breath. "Sorry, Nick. I was laughing when I answered."

"Well, I'll just assume you are happy to be working for me."

"I am."

"Good. Rick Rosenberg from Rosenberg Restoration is the project manager. He can meet you there at nine tomorrow to go over the project. According to Rick, there are specific paints that should be used. Also, you'll need to see if you can work with him since he is your real boss."

"Do you normally get this involved in your projects?"

"This one is special, so I am more involved than usual. Don't worry, though. I won't be sticking my nose in too much, and other than when I am already scheduled to be in the area, I won't be dropping in."

"Wasn't exactly worried about that." If she knew Nick better, Candace would have brought up the subject of her cousin. Zoe's calls and texts had been too vague on the subject of Nick.

"At the moment I don't intend to be in the Chicago area until Daniel's New Year's party."

"Hopefully in four months there will be something to show you."

"I look forward to it."

The call ended. Candace used her phone to capture a photo of the flowers.

Her thumb hovered over the Send button. The photo was funny, but it might be seen as making fun of Colin. Candace hit the trash icon instead and sent a different message.

Candace: Took the job. Colin sent me flowers to congratulate me.

Mandy: Photo?

Candace: Sorry. A photo won't do these flowers justice.

Tessa: Has he ever sent you flowers before?

Candace: No. But they were just a way of saying congrats. But since he is also taking me out to dinner, unnecessary.

Abbie: Flowers are never unnecessary.

Candace: I'd better get ready.

Mandy: Have fun at dinner.

Candace checked her makeup in the mirror and reapplied eyebrow pencil. She must have rubbed some of it off during the drive. She was already wearing one of her natural colored wigs since she didn't know who she might meet looking at the warehouse, and spiky pink hair or a plumb bob wasn't always the best first impression. Colin hadn't taken her out before, at least not alone. He wasn't paralyzed in social situations; however, he probably didn't need people staring at her hair and then at him. She was used to the stares, although the last couple years as more women colored their hair in tones of blue and crimson, fewer strangers stopped to look. However, Colin shunned attention, and so she kept the plain wig on.

The doorbell rang, and Candace's heart sped up. She took a calming breath, telling herself it was silly to get worked up over Colin.

Colin smoothed the front of his plaid shirt—not too laid back like his favorite T-shirts, yet it didn't require a tie. Finding his hands were sweaty, he was shoving them into his jean pockets to wipe them off just as Candace answered the door. She wore the same understated wig she had at Tessa's wedding.

"Come in."

Part of the hallway was blocked by a giant display of flowers. He carefully edged around them.

"Thank you for the flowers. Would you help me move them over by the window?"

"I sent you these?"

Candace raised one painted brow at him. "The card was signed, or rather typed, 'Colin.' So I assume they are from you. Didn't you order them?"

"Sabrina did."

"Is there something I should know about Sabrina?"

"She is the AI I told you I was working on." Sabrina was in for some serious reprogramming.

"The home-helper thing? Sorry to say this, but I think she failed this task. Or she is trying to send one of us a message." Candace smiled and pointed to the other side of the arrangement. "Lift that side. Let's put it to the right of the sliding door."

"I haven't programmed Sabrina with any dark humor, so I am hoping it was just a misunderstanding."

"At least she got the color right, and it does smell nice."

Her smile didn't make him feel any better about the blunder. Even he would have chosen something that didn't look like a funeral spray. "I'm sorry. I meant it to be more like the ones Daniel sent Mandy after the internet blew up with the dating stuff."

"Those flowers were impressive. But I like what you sent."

"You don't need to make me feel better about the mistake." *Colossal blunder*. Colin wanted to knock himself in the head. Funeral flowers. After their conversation on the plane, he had been stupid enough to let Sabrina order the flowers. Even a bridal bouquet would have been better.

"I'm not, unless it turns out this job doesn't work for me. Then I would have to call it a sign."

"I'm really sorry. I can get you something else." Next time he would just order a dozen roses. Even an AI couldn't get that wrong. But the wrong color could send a message that would be worse than funeral arrangements. No wonder Daniel used to have Bonnie order flowers for him. It would be worth the consulting fee to order the right flowers next time.

Candace patted his arm. "They wouldn't be nearly as memorable. But there are some things you might not want to leave to your AI."

"I tried to ask for dinner recommendations, and Sabrina—" He couldn't tell her about the date recipes or she would know this was a date.

"Recommended the golden arches?"

His phone vibrated. "Something like that. Are you ready? My chauffeur is downstairs."

Candace nodded.

Colin wasn't sure if he should offer her his arm since this was a date, but he decided against it. His palms were sweaty again anyway. He hoped the evening wouldn't get any worse than the funeral flowers.

Mr. Alexander stood in the lobby, his muscled arms bulging under his short-sleeved polo shirt, a frown on his face. Alexander Hastings, Alex to his friends and Mr. to his clients, headed Daniel Crawford's security team.

Candace stopped short. "Is something wrong, Alex?"

"Nothing we can't solve. Mr. Crawford informed me Mr. Ogilvie forgot to put a security detail in place for his night out. Where were you planning on going?"

Colin mumbled the name of the restaurant like a teenage boy caught sneaking out his window. A security detail was an everyday occurrence for most billionaires, but Colin wasn't most. His reclusive lifestyle meant he spent most of his time at home or in the office. Any social events he attended were usually in the company of Daniel, who had a full detail at all times. Work-related events were handled by the office, and his mother's people dealt with family things. Candace must think he was a dork not to have even thought about it.

"At least you chose someplace easy. Tell your driver to take the long route to give me time to get there." Alex opened the door to the stairwell and had descended half the steps to the parking garage before the door shut behind him.

"I am a bit rusty at this go-to-the-food thing. I usually just order in." Colin waited while Candace got into the car. "I guess I need to remember to tell someone my plans."

"I've only seen you out with Daniel and his team. Do you even have a head of your personal security?"

"I must. I just have never thought about it." He leaned forward to talk to the driver. "Jim, do I have a head of security?"

"You have me, sir. For most of your activities I am enough, but I can't call in full detail. That must be requested from Hastings."

"Oh. Thanks." Colin sat back. "I guess I do."

Candace laid her hand on his arm. Every hair stood at attention. "I am glad you don't have to spend too much time worrying about it."

Maybe they could skip the restaurant. Sitting in the back seat with Candace was enough for him. And he wouldn't have to worry about a security detail or the other people at the restaurant. Next time he would choose something much less public. Only that might not be a good idea. Hadn't he read something about a woman's need to be seen publicly with a man? It didn't matter how much Nick or Daniel had helped him, the sense of impending doom that Colin would mess up this dating attempt followed him into the restaurant.

eight

SATURDAY AFTERNOON, CANDACE TURNED THE thermostat at Art House to sixty degrees. It was the last thing on her to-do list to close the place for the winter. Closing the house just as fall semester started seemed just as surreal as her date two nights ago with Colin. He hadn't called it a date. Neither of them had, but it felt like one. Butterflies in the stomach, awkward moments of silence during the meal. The uncomfortable moment as he dropped her off at her apartment before she gave him a friendly hug.

SHE GRABBED HER PURSE OFF the kitchen table—the table where they'd met a year and a half ago or so by video call. She had immediately felt a zing of attraction for the nerdy guy with the glasses, which he hadn't been wearing as often lately. With Mandy dating his best friend and business partner, Colin had been quickly removed from her list of possible guys to date. He was too close to Daniel, and she would end up seeing Colin again and again. An awkward situation she preferred to avoid. It was about the time she realized the folly of part of her bucket list and stopped dating guys just so she could get to number ten. But did she want the other night to be a date? If so, was she admitting she had a future? Too many questions and not enough answers.

Candace did one last walk through to make sure she hadn't missed anything she might need in Chicago. Even though she'd be only three hours away, she didn't want to be running back and forth constantly. She turned off the last light and shut the door as a sadness she couldn't quite identify welled up in her. Although the Art House would always be a significant part of her life, she felt she would never be a major part of the house's history again.

The alarm beeped after Candace keyed in the enabling code. Mandy had insisted on having Hastings security add a few measures to monitor the empty house and help it not look so empty, which included hiring a lawn service. She would miss raking leaves in a couple weeks, but not picking up the black walnut shells or shoveling the snow after one of Northern Indiana's storms. The nice thing was that she could come back whenever she wanted and the house would be ready. Candace had argued with Mandy over who was going to foot the bill and cost after Mandy paid it a year in advance.

There was barely enough room in the car for Candace to sit and be able to see out the rearview mirror. Dawdling any longer would only get her stuck in Chicago's rush hour, so she cut across Northern Indiana using some of the back roads, passing a couple horse-drawn carts laden with hay bales outside Goshen. She was within a couple of miles of the farm she'd grown up on. Her uncle now owned the land that had been passed down from generation to generation of Wilsons. Some of the earliest settlers had come to Indiana shortly after the War of 1812. Candace didn't stop, knowing it was impossible to stay for only five minutes where her aunt was concerned. Zoe's mother would, no doubt, have some new story she'd learned about some ancestor that would take twice as long to tell as the actual occurrence. Candace would rather wait until Thanksgiving, when Zoe would also be there to listen to family lore.

As always, the traffic congestion near Chicago slowed her journey. In the year since Mandy had moved there, Candace had made the trip dozens of times. But this was the first time she found her stomach full of butterflies. She was starting a new project, although she hadn't made a new plan. Yet this project was at least a year commitment. In the past six months she had turned down several projects because the commitments would have taken her too far past the end of her ten-year plan. Maybe she should do as Reverend Cavanagh advised and plan on living. She was turning a corner—of that she was sure. Bucket-list items filled her mind, though most of them weren't as exciting as they should have been. Reading fifty-two books over the next year was one of her favorites. She'd never been much of a reader, but Araceli's love of books inspired her. She could start by reading the books her roommates had chosen to signal the others they would be using the loft above the library and were not to be disturbed. Dubbed "Lover's Loft" by one of her first roommates, it had been most recently used to make long-distance phone calls by both Tessa and Araceli.

Her thoughts turned to the other items she had contemplated. The bucket-list goal she'd made when she was sixteen of kissing a new guy every year had missed the mark—a deeper connection she hadn't realized she could or should make until she'd watched her roommates this past year with their boyfriends, now husbands. Instead of choosing a number of men to kiss, she vowed to never kiss another man she didn't have a deep connection with.

At the moment, there was only one man who might be a candidate. Colin. And it seemed she was trying to be a candidate too. Of course, the bouquet he had given her the night of the congratulatory dinner would have looked more at home in a funeral parlor than it did next to the window in her apartment. She smiled. Only Colin would let his household AI order flowers without giving the computer proper parameters.

Her cell rang an old Barry Manilow song. It had been a joke to use Mandy's namesake song, as their friendship had nothing in common with the love ballad. The song drove Mandy crazy. Candace answered it through the car system.

"Hey, when will you be here?"

"I am only two miles away, but traffic is moving slowly."

"Okay, I have pizza and some help—in the form of Abbie and her brothers, Daniel, and Colin. We should have you unloaded in ten minutes or less."

"Sounds like a party." Candace wasn't sure she wanted witnesses to her move. Her mind raced through the boxes and bags in her car. She was pretty sure anything unmentionable was out of sight. Only one box might be a problem, but she should be able to quickly get it in her laundry basket.

"We'll see you in a few. Just send me a text when you get into the garage."

"Will do."

The attendant nodded as she opened the gate to the underground garage. As soon as she parked, she hopped out and popped the trunk. The box of unmentionables sat next to her large suitcase. She'd just finished rearranging when her friends poured out of the elevator bay.

Mandy balanced Joy on her hip. "You were supposed to text."

"I was just making sure all my girly things were not out in the open."

Both Mandy and Colin reddened at the comment.

"So is it safe to unload?" asked Abbie.

"If it isn't, just close your eyes and pretend you didn't see anything."

The Hasting brothers had a couple of dollies with them. In just one trip, the friends managed to unload everything she'd spent hours packing into the car.

Candace would be far from lonely living alone for the first time in her life. Looking around the room at all her friends eating pizza, a glimpse of life beyond Art House flickered in her heart. Five-year reunions would be a necessity. She could do a five-year plan.

"Sabrina, what is today?"

"Today is Thursday, September 20. You have two projects over-due. One, beta testing of app version number seven on project Abbie. Two, take Candace on a second date. Would you like suggestions?"

"No, thank you." 532 days. He was not going to take any advice from the AI who'd ordered the flowers for Candace. Alex had knocked them over when they were moving Candace into the apartment, and the whole embarrassing story had come out. Daniel offered lessons on choosing flowers. Candace jumped to his defense, but it hadn't kept him from wishing he was alone in his apartment. Well, alone with Candace.

He had no idea what to do. In desperation, he texted Nick.

Help—need a date idea for Candace.

—Have you been to the theater?

No, I don't have any idea what movie to take her to.

—Not a movie theater. Plays or musicals.

Like Les Mis**?**

—Like that, and don't forget the tickets for the security detail.

Hey, it was a first date.

—At least you are relatively unknown. I can never forget them.

It is taking some getting used to. Hastings had assigned Andrew to him. The youngest of the brothers was easy to get along with and seemed to understand Colin's introvert tendencies.

—How does Candace deal with security? I think mine freaked Zoe out a bit.

She knows the Hastings security team better than I do. So not a problem. Any suggestions on shows?

—Wicked, Hamilton—**any of the classics. Check reviews. Some shows get explicit or have onstage nudity.**

Really? I thought it was all Sound of Music **stuff.**

—**Have you asked Daniel's old secretary, the one who was playing grandma at the wedding, for dating advice?**

Good idea. Later.

Colin dialed Bonnie's number.

"Colin? Is something wrong?"

"Not really. I just need help with a date." This was only slightly less embarrassing than calling his mother.

"With Candace?" The surprise in her voice was poorly masked.

"Yes, my friend suggested the theater, but—"

"When do you want to go?"

"This weekend?"

"You know the popular shows sell out weeks in advance, don't you?"

"They do?"

"Let me take care of it. Two-person security team as well?"

"Is that what Daniel did?"

"Yes. Have you asked her?"

"No?"

Bonnie's laughter filled the phone. "Give me an hour, and I'll text you. Then you can ask. Anything else?"

"Did you hear about the funeral flowers?"

"A little bird may have said something about them. Next time take her a single pink rose. Work your way up to red."

The advice was exactly what he was looking for. "Thanks, Bonnie."

"Only for you, but don't make a habit of it, okay?"

"No problem." He disconnected and prepared himself one of Janie's meals while he waited.

"Sabrina—best ways to ask a woman on a date?"

"According to the first article, a man should avoid the D word."

"Sabrina, *D*?"

"*Date.*"

"Sabrina, how do you ask someone out for a date without saying *date*?"

"That search returned no results."

"Sabrina, search tips for asking a woman out."

"One: be confident. Two: call, don't text. Three: be clear you are asking her out."

Well, that wasn't very helpful. So much easier to be confident when texting and being vague.

"Sabrina, turn on the Hearthfire channel."

Perhaps he could find some inspiration. But he had already seen this one. Not his situation at all.

"Sabrina, turn off the TV."

His phone pinged.

—Four tickets, Saturday 8:00 p.m. show. Driver and security detail scheduled. Would you like dinner at six?

Thanks, Bonnie. Dinner would be nice.

—Enjoy the show.

Before he could think too much, he called Candace.

"Hi, Colin, what's up?"

"Hi, I just—" *Realized that Bonnie didn't tell me what show.* He couldn't find the words to continue.

"Colin? Are you okay?"

A funny little gasp came out of his throat.

"I'm coming up!" The call ended.

"Sabrina, let her come up in the elevator."

"Define *her*."

"Candace Wilson."

"Allowing Candace Wilson access to the penthouse suite."

Candace rushed out of the elevator. "Oh, thank goodness. I thought you had passed out."

"Nothing so traumatic."

She took his hand and led him over to the couch. "Why did you call?"

Colin took a deep breath. "I called to ask you out to dinner and the theater."

"Oh."

That was it? Wasn't she supposed to say yes? What had he done wrong? His mind raced for something to say, but it was stuck on "oh" too.

nine

Date.

Candace turned the word over, exploring it like hard candy, testing the flavor to see if it was sweet or bitter. Saying yes to Colin was riskier than to any other guy who'd asked her out. There was friendship on the line.

From the earnest look on Colin's face, a no would put an end to the friendship sooner.

"What time should I be ready?" She twirled the end of the scarf she'd tied around her head as she'd run out of the apartment. Oddly, Colin hadn't even commented on her headwear. Most people did comment the first time they saw her without hair. Of course, he had seen her in a scarf on video call, but this was the first in real life. And he was more concerned about asking her out than her lack of follicles.

His eyes lit up. "Five thirty? I'll take you to dinner before the show."

"What show?" Candace wondered if it would be one she hadn't seen yet.

His face pinked. "I wasn't sure how to get tickets…"

"Please tell me you didn't ask Sabrina for help."

"No, I asked Bonnie."

A safe option. Bonnie wouldn't pick something awful. "She wouldn't tell you where you are going?"

"She texted me the time but not the show. I called you and realized I didn't know what I was asking you out for." His voice trailed off. That explained why he had frozen on the call.

"You could text her now and ask."

"I could, but Bonnie might not answer. You know how she was with Daniel and Mandy." She made Daniel deal with his problems himself, causing any number of problems. "I'm surprised she helped me. Although it could be a high school production."

"It will still be fun. Some high school shows are brilliant."

"Really? I've never been to one."

"Not surprising. The school you went to wasn't exactly typical."

He rubbed his forehead. "I know—the whole boarding-school thing."

She didn't express her thoughts on the matter. Families should stay together, and sending eleven-year-olds to live with other preteens did not make for strong familial bonds.

"What else are you going to do tonight?" Candace thought of the empty apartment downstairs and realized she didn't want to go back.

"I don't know. I have an app to work on. I thought of watching a show, but all I found was a rerun."

"Don't you have streaming?"

"Oh yeah. I forgot about that." Probably because he was always thinking of the next project. "Do you want to do something with me? Like we can play a game. I have chess."

"I don't think I stand a chance at chess. Maybe I can introduce you to a new show." Anything Candace picked that wasn't sci-fi should be new to him. Not a bad thing. Colin never made time to watch TV and, as a result, was the most productive person she knew.

"Sabrina, turn on the TV and bring up streaming."

A list of channels appeared on the screen as the TV sprang to life. "Which streaming channel?" The computer voice asked the question without inflection.

Colin shrugged and turned to Candace.

She looked up at the ceiling, where the voice came from. "Sabrina, the Hearthfire channel."

The screen didn't change

"What did I say wrong?"

"Nothing. Sabrina has a voice-recognition feature. She only responds to my voice. We can teach her to recognize yours."

"How do we do that?"

"When I give the AI the command and she says 'Ready,' you will say, 'Sabrina, this is Candace' five times. It helps if you change the inflection in your voice from fast to slow to angry, etc." Colin opened an app on his phone.

"Sabrina, program new voice recognition."

"Ready for input," said the computer voice.

"Sabrina, this is Candace." She tried to keep her voice as even as possible. Then she tried an annoyed-sounding voice since she figured if she talked to the AI often, she would be annoyed. By the time she hit her fifth "Sabrina, this is Candace," she was laughing hard.

"I'm not sure that last one took." Colin typed into his phone. "Now try asking her for the channel you want."

"Sabrina, Hearthfire channel."

The channel appeared on the large TV screen.

"Yes!" Colin punched the air. "You are in!"

"Of course I'm in. You wouldn't design something that didn't work."

"Funeral flowers."

He had a point there, but he had thought of buying flowers, which she doubted he had ever done before. "That wasn't your design. It was lack of input data." Colin never gave himself enough credit. It was one of the few things that annoyed her about him.

Colin watched the rom-com with only half interest. Candace hadn't moved over when he'd sat next to her on the couch. According to everything he'd read, he should hold her hand next. Unlike with Dora Greenwood when he was thirteen, he wanted to hold Candace's hand.

During the scene where the guy finally noticed the girl, Colin's pinky touched Candace's. She didn't move away, so he slid his hand over and watched how it covered hers, his thumb involuntarily rubbing the back of her knuckles—not the reaction he'd expected. Candace moved an inch closer, and his chest swelled with warmth. Strange … none of the articles he'd read included that reaction.

Candace's fingers moved in a duet with his, the TV noise becoming background to the new feelings he was experiencing. The music swelled before the credits rolled. As he had programmed them to, the lights in the room brightened slowly.

Candace sat and pulled away. "Sabrina, what time is it? "

"10:26 p.m."

"I should go. I am starting to paint the upper mural tomorrow. If I don't get enough sleep, sometimes my hands don't want to work right."

"May I walk you down?"

"The stairs?" A soft, teasing smile graced her lips.

"Ten flights? I thought the elevator would be better."

She nodded.

The trip down lasted only a few seconds. He wondered if he could install a variable-speed mechanism in the elevator. At the moment, he would prefer a snail's pace over the standard high speed of the penthouse elevator. Maybe he could push every button like a little kid. But that would mean other people could get on.

The elevator dinged at her floor. Colin had Candace exit first but didn't let go of her hand. Her apartment door wasn't exactly like the front porches from the scenes in the Hearthfire movies he had been studying. The fluorescent lights of the hallway were anything but romantic. How was he to attempt a first kiss here?

"Thanks for letting me barge in and stay." Candace dropped her hand and unlocked her door.

"Thanks for running up and rescuing me from my blunder."

Candace turned to face him. "Good night, Colin." She rose up on her toes and kissed his cheek.

Frozen in place, he watched her enter the apartment and close the door.

Candace had just kissed him.

He needed to move. What if she was watching his reaction through the peephole? He returned to the elevator and went straight to the penthouse level, where he pushed the fingerprint-scanning button.

Once in the penthouse foyer, he paused. Just how did one go about kissing the most incredible woman in the world? If only he hadn't spent so much time figuring out computers at school.

Watching the twenty-five best movie kisses according to Sabrina didn't help either. The only one that made much sense to him was the animated dogs kissing over a plate of pasta. Grab-a-girl-and-kiss-her-silly wasn't his style. Apparently kissing wasn't something he could read about and learn.

Maybe for now he would stick with holding hands. That act evoked sensations he had not anticipated. Holding hands was good. It was more than good. It was stupendous.

ten

Joy yawned and frowned in her sleep, and Candace adjusted her hold on Mandy's baby. "She is so sweet."

"No fair using my daughter to deflect. I was asking about Colin." Mandy sat in the other chair. "If you don't tell me now, I'll call you at 2:00 a.m. when she is screaming her head off, and you can deal with her not-so-sweet moments."

"I thought we needed to discuss the Hearthfire showing in Blue Pines." Candace tried to change the subject again.

"Nice try. Tessa and I have that under control. I'll go out in October to make final arrangements. But that is not the point. Spill, or I let the little one scream you awake."

Candace adjusted the blanket around Joy's face. "Don't say such disparaging things about my honorary niece. You exaggerate."

"About her crying, or me calling you with it?"

"Both, but I'll tell you anyway. Colin officially asked me on a date. Even got Bonnie to help him with the arrangements."

"What are you doing?"

Candace stifled a laugh, not wanting to wake Joy. "Colin was a bit vague on that. Bonnie didn't give him the name of the play or musical she got tickets for. I think he is afraid to ask her."

Mandy covered her mouth with her hand. After a moment, she removed it. "Let me go put her in her crib so we can laugh."

Candace sat down in her favorite chair. A few boxes stood against the wall. Daniel and Mandy's new house was finished. They decided they would rather not raise Joy in the heart of the city, but they would keep the penthouse for events there.

Mandy returned in a different shirt. "Joy gave me a little good-night spit up. I am not sure the pumpkin spice cake I had this morning agreed with her. Now, back to Colin and Bonnie. She probably didn't tell him just to get him to make his own dates. Nothing annoyed her more than when Daniel would ask for her help in his personal matters. Of course, with me, it is a different story. I don't think I can ask too many silly personal questions, as long I ask them between the hours of nine and eleven in the morning." Mandy took a seat in the chair opposite her. "Although I can pretty much text her anytime of day with a Joy-related question. Now, I digress. What did you think of Colin asking you out?"

"It was inevitable?"

"That is not what I mean."

"Honestly, I have never been so nervous about a date in my life. With my ten-year plan, I never took any guy very seriously. He was just fun for the moment. Colin is different. We have been talking and doing things together for a year and a half, but it has almost always been in the context of doing them with you and Daniel or because of the other roommates. I am comfortable with where things have been. He knows me as well as many of my roommates do."

"Have you told him about the ten-year plan?"

"A little, but not the real pain behind it. There was a point I honestly didn't think I would live for ten years—or if I wanted to. I lost so much."

"How long was it after your mom died that your dad figured out you had become addicted to pain pills?"

"He didn't. It was my sister. Somehow in the middle of everything, she had gotten engaged to a med student, of all things. I was barely talking to her I was so mad about Mom dying. I think her fiancé noticed it first and pushed her into telling Dad and confronting me. The fact that other than my mother's pain-pill stash I had gotten the rest legally blew everyone's mind. Some of the doctors were on a different computer system, and since some prescriptions were filled in Houston and others in Indianapolis, the pharmacy hadn't realized what I was doing either."

"Does Colin know?"

"I told him last fall. It came up one day about why I was so adamant about not having painkillers around when I was using an ice pack for a headache." Ice worked relatively fast for her.

"How hard was it when I broke my foot and had the painkillers in the house?"

"You mean your lover's fracture?" Candace loved using the nickname of the type of break Mandy had received from falling off Daniel's fence, especially since the name turned out to be somewhat prophetic. "I was surprised how easy it was to leave them alone."

"That's good. I always worried about that. Have you told Colin everything else?"

"You mean the full effects of the cancer? Not yet. If our dating looks like we are moving forward, I will tell him then. In the meantime, he knows enough. You know, he doesn't treat me any differently when I am wearing a scarf than when I am wearing a wig. I'm not sure if it's because he doesn't notice what I am wearing or if he really doesn't care."

"I think he notices. Colin said he had a favorite wig."

"Really? Which one?"

"I think you need to ask him that." Mandy smiled one of those annoying I-know-what-is-best smiles.

Candace decided to change the topic again. "Did I tell you Zoe went to the 9/11-wing opening at the museum?"

"She sent photos to the group chat, and Tessa posted too. Is it my imagination, or is Zoe mentioning Nick a lot?"

Nick would be so right for her cousin. Sean vouched that his childhood friend had earned the nickname "Do-Gooding." "I have noticed that too. To be honest, I didn't know if she would choose to move on, even with all the support she has had this past year. Statistically, the majority of men are decent people, even if they do seem to be from another planet sometimes."

"I like Nick. Daniel was talking about some of the things they did in school together. Nick is pretty good-natured and can handle a joke. Did Colin tell you about hacking Nick's computer?"

"No."

"It was like their junior year, and Nick's dad bought him this new wireless printer. Colin realized it wasn't protected and started sending documents to it. Things like, 'Hi, Nick, I liked your striped socks today.' 'Nick, please remove the yellow toner. She is bringing cyan down.' 'Stop ignoring me, or I will not print that term paper you are working on.'"

Candace held her sides to keep the laughter from hurting her ribs. "No way. What did Nick do?"

"He took the printer to Colin and told him it was creepily self-aware and asked Colin to fix it. Colin told him it might be expensive and got a month's worth of cleanup dorm duties in exchange. Then, a couple days before the end of their senior year, Colin sent a message to the printer confessing about the open Wi-Fi and that he'd hacked the printer. Daniel said he hadn't seen Nick laugh so hard as when he told the story of his self-aware printer."

"That would freak me out! 'Hi, I am your printer, and I am self-aware.' I would chuck it into the nearest dumpster. Then, when I found out, I would be so annoyed." Practical jokes. Colin didn't seem the type, which made it all the funnier. Candace and Mandy laughed until tears formed. "At least I'll know now if my printer starts acting up it has been hacked." Part of her wished he would, just so she could see the humorous side of him. Suddenly she couldn't wait for Saturday's date.

Concentrating on the board meeting was harder than usual. Colin never cared about the nontech side of the business. It was a good thing he had Daniel for a partner. Fortunately, Colin's tech inventions made them enough money that Daniel was more than happy to deal with the mundane and day to day. But this meeting, instead of thinking of the line of code he could adjust, he was thinking of Candace. Perhaps it was the scarf Mrs. Johnson, one of the board members, wore. The soft colors were not Candace's style, yet he thought of how the soft pastels would make her eyes sparkle.

When the meeting concluded, Colin shook all the hands he needed to and breathed a sigh of relief when only Daniel remained.

"Whatever the new idea you have in mind is, it must be good. You haven't been that out of it in a board meeting for a while."

Colin removed his tie. "Sorry about that."

"What is the idea?"

"It wasn't an app. I asked Candace out on a real date."

Daniel stopped shuffling the papers in front of him. "As in you said 'I am asking you on a date' and not just one of those sideways-slide, hanging-out-with-her things?"

"I lost it on the phone. I think she thought I was going into shock. I couldn't say a word."

"But she still said yes?"

"After she came up to the penthouse to check on me and I explained. I should have paid more attention to girls in school. I have no idea how to do this."

Daniel nodded in the direction of his office. Colin followed him down the hall to one of the corner offices, where Daniel shut the door behind them. "Are you asking for advice?"

"Maybe?" Colin had no idea what might help relieve the stress building inside him.

"You two have been friends for a long time. Just hold on to that. Have you ever run out of things to talk about?"

"No. Not yet."

"Then it probably won't happen during your date, either. I know your mother drilled proper etiquette into you so much that Miss Manners herself would have a hard time finding something you don't know. Fall back on that if all else fails." Nick hung his suit coat in the closet.

Colin sat on the arm of one of the plush chairs. "I don't know that etiquette can save me."

"Sure it can. Offer your arm and ask a question. Trust me. That will give you a few more minutes to collect yourself."

"Candace has an uncanny way of turning things back on me."

"Ask about art. It works with Mandy every time." Daniel smiled.

"You need time to think when you are around your wife?"

"Occasionally I am thinking about a business problem or too much about Mandy, and I need a moment."

Colin wondered how someone could think about their wife too much, then realization hit him, and he hoped his neck wasn't turning red.

Daniel smiled. His best friend had meant to bait him. "Any other pointers?"

Colin shook his head. No way was he going to ask Daniel about how one knew it was time to kiss. The chances that it would get repeated at an inopportune time were too high. "How do I get Bonnie to tell me where we are going?"

"You had Bonnie set up your date?"

"I didn't know how to get tickets."

Daniel whistled. "You are one brave soul. Fortunately for you, she likes Candace, and you were not a goof-up in college like I was, so you don't have to worry. This time."

"I thought about that. I am going to need to come up with my own dates."

"I can help with that. Let me think of some, and I'll text them to you."

"Thanks." *I think.* Daniel's dating ideas could be as dangerous as having Bonnie arrange his dates. Which brought him back full circle to his problem—tomorrow night's date.

eleven

BONNIE HAD COME THROUGH WITH flying colors—seats at the sold-out Broadway tour show, quiet table for two in an upscale restaurant. The most surprising thing was they had reached intermission and Colin hadn't pulled out a phone or tablet once. He also didn't seem to be going through withdrawals. Of course, he had spent the entire first act using his fingers to explore her hand and wrist. Candace had no idea she had so many sensitive nerve endings in those places. She'd held a few guys hands before, but it was always about the goal of getting to the kiss or something that would get the guy slapped.

He traced the little scar on the back of her hand from one of the many IV lines that had been placed there. It wasn't the only scar left from her cancer years, but it was the easiest to see. Yet few ever noticed. Colin noticed little things. Other than Mandy and Zoe, she didn't feel like many people, even those she called friends, saw her under her crazy wigs and bright artist colors. Colin was coming dangerously close.

The music changed to a melancholy tune as the wise-old-man character sang a ballad. Something about him reminded her of Reverend Cavanagh. Would he be proud she'd started a ten-year plan? She would finish the carousel and convince Nick to use it to open an indoor theme park for children with cancer. Many rides would need to be relatively tame, like the merry-go-round, to accommodate those who might bruise easily from faster rides because of blood conditions. Rigorous sanitation standards would be the most difficult thing to maintain. The rides would need to be cleaned often. Not to mention the need to accommodate oxygen tanks and other medical equipment. The idea kept turning around in her head. Things like fair games that were possible to win, unlike a shooting gallery, could be modified so as to be accessible to wheelchair-reliant patients.

A tingling sensation in her arm brought her thoughts back to another thing in her new plan. A deep and meaningful relationship.

Colin's fingers trailed up and down her arm, and a tiny sigh escaped her. If only the show could go on and on. Out of the corner of her eye, she caught him looking at her instead of at the stage, where one of the greatest performances of the decade was rapidly drawing to a close. She smiled at him, and he turned his attention back to the show. Candace used her other hand to trace a pattern on the back of his. Only as she started the second time through the pattern did she realize it resembled a Celtic love knot.

She paused. Meaningful relationship didn't mean she needed to be in love, did it? It must be just leftover thoughts from so many of her friends getting married this year. One could have a deep relationship without falling in love—or maybe a man and woman couldn't. Her thoughts ebbed and flowed with the song to the finale. Too bad real life couldn't be solved with a song. If she kept going out with Colin, she was just setting him up to be hurt. Over the past year and a half, she'd gleaned that Colin may not have dated anyone in his life. At least not that Daniel knew of. She should just end it now.

But the little electrical sparks traveling up her arm and making their way to nudge her heart begged her not to. Did a meaningful relationship mean there would be pain?

As the theater started to clear, Colin stood and helped Candace with the light wrap she'd brought. There was something sad about her smile. Perhaps she found the end of the musical as moving as he had. Musical theater went on his list of activities to do again, preferably with Candace.

When the room was three-quarters empty, Andrew Hastings approached from the wings. "There is a great deal of paparazzi out front due to a particular singing sensation in the audience. If you come this way, we can use a rear exit."

Colin tucked Candace's hand into the crook of his arm like he did when escorting a dance partner to the floor, then followed Andrew out of the building. The other security guard followed them.

Once they were securely in the car, Colin resumed holding Candace's hand. Sometime during the past forty-eight hours, he'd concluded that hand-holding was underestimated in every article he ever read. It was far more intimate than given credit for. He could die quite happily now.

"I had no idea the theater could be so exciting. I guess I shouldn't have dodged my mother's invitations all these years." Now that his father had passed, he wished he had taken the time to get to know his parents better, but they didn't understand him any more than they did his love for programming. Mother's interest in his life had increased exponentially since Daniel's wedding last year, the interest mostly manifested in not-so-cleverly-disguised attempts to set him up with her friends' daughters. He wondered what his mother would think of Candace. They'd met, of course, at Daniel's wedding and again at the New Year's party. But both times, Candace had been dressed what his mother would call "appropriately," meaning Candace's hair wasn't green, or pink, or orange.

Candace asked him a question. He had been so distracted with his own thoughts he had to ask her to repeat it.

"I asked what your favorite part was."

Holding your hand. "The dancing at the beginning of the second part."

"That was good. I want to try a couple of those moves."

"Come dancing with me next weekend."

"Where?"

"I am sure we can find something. If not, there is the ballroom out at the house. We can go there. Mother won't mind if she is there." She would be delighted. All week he'd dodged her calls, knowing she was curious about the date. Janie must have blabbed.

"You have a ballroom?" She sat up straight and turned to him. "Why have you not told me this?"

"It never came up?" No way was he ready to take Candace out to the house if his mother was around. Mom would be contacting her calligrapher for the wedding invitations.

"In all the dancing we have done, it never came up?" Candace shook her head and sat back, leaning into his side. "We have been friends for a year and a half. What other secrets do you have?"

I've never kissed a woman, and I want to kiss you. "I don't know. There is also a swimming pool with a removable structure so it is open year around. I just don't think about things like that."

The driver pulled into the underground parking lot and stopped in front of the elevator bay.

"Do you want to come up? I asked Sabrina to put ice cream on the order. And I was very specific about it being chocolate with fudge ribbons." Colin held his breath, waiting for the answer.

"Sure. If your AI goofed, I have some of the good stuff at my apartment." Candace entered the elevator with him.

He might have tried to kiss her then, but he knew the security camera would catch the moment, and no way would Hastings Security get an image of his first kiss.

This time he didn't mind that the elevator was in express mode.

twelve

SABRINA GOT THE ICE CREAM order correct after only four tries. The AI earned her keep today. Candace scooped a bowl of cookies and cream for Colin and one of double chocolate fudge for herself while he got them both a glass of water. She set the ice cream on the table.

Colin picked up his bowl. "It is a clear night. Let's go eat in the observatory."

Candace followed him up a stairway and then a spiral staircase that reminded her of the one in Art House. Only, instead of a cramped loft, it led to a room with three-quarter walls and a glass roof. Music played softly from hidden speakers. Colin took a seat on the leather sofa. She sat next to him. The light from two buildings over shone through the south window.

"Sabrina, close the south binds up to point B on the roof."

Within seconds the space between the panes was filled with a solid-looking substance blocking out the light.

"Those aren't normal blinds, are they?" Candace winced at her obvious observation.

"It is an invention I have been working on, but it still has issues. It heats up too much in the summer sun, so I have a set of exterior metal blinds that cover the room when not in use. The glass offers

UV protection—not that it is an issue at night." Colin continued into the more technical aspects of the substance in the windows.

Candace ate her ice cream and nodded whenever she grasped a point.

Colin paused. "Sorry, I went a bit overboard there. I guess you didn't need to know the chemical makeup of it, did you?"

"I like how passionate you get about your projects. I don't need to understand everything to enjoy it."

"Finished with your ice cream?" Colin held out his hand, and she passed him her bowl. He crossed the room and set them in a small dumbwaiter, then returned to her. "Now, for the show."

The sofa began to recline until she was almost prone. With any other guy, Candace would wonder if she was being seduced.

"Sabrina, artificial light filters." The electric glow that defined Chicago at night dimmed. Light from stars rarely seen in the city twinkled through the windows.

"Oh, wow. I never thought I would see the Big Dipper in the heart of the city." Candace pointed northward.

"There is Mars. Tomorrow is the autumnal equinox. Fall will really be here." Colin slid his head closer to hers and pointed. "That is Taurus."

"Pumpkin-spice time can officially begin!" Candace refused to start fall a day early, even if the stores had.

"Just as long as you don't eat that pumpkin-spice cereal."

She turned to him. "They have cereal?"

"Don't get too excited. It might be good if it were oatmeal based, but the stuff Janie bought for me tastes pretty bad. I have most of the box left if you want to try some, but I did warn you." His face relaxed as it did when he moved to topics that were not computer or invention related.

"My favorites are the donuts and pumpkin-blueberry muffins. I usually make a batch or two to share with my roommates so I don't eat them all."

"I can eat a few."

"I'll bring some up, then. I can take some to my coworkers. Maybe that will help them not think I am so odd."

"Odd? Why would they think that? How is work going?"

"My end is easy, but I work alone at this point. I may bring an intern in next semester. Everyone else is working on the restoration. Some of the paint on the carousel has lead in it, and some of the colors have pigments that are now banned or considered unsafe, like uranium yellow and Scheele's green."

"Whoa, someone made paint out of uranium? Wouldn't that be radioactive?" Colin rolled over and propped his head on his arm.

"It was a popular color for centuries. Women who were helping in the World War II war effort would roll the tips of their brushes in their mouths, and many got cancer. All of what they have found here is registering at very low levels on a Geiger counter, so low it's well below EPA standards. However, since children will be using this, there is a yellow bench a master carpenter is rebuilding from scratch. In places where the yellow can be removed, it is being replaced with a safer, slightly less-vibrant color."

"So what about the green?"

"The emerald-green color contains arsenic and is everywhere on the carousel. The color was trendy until about 1900. It was in clothing, wallpaper, and on children's toys. People died from it. The restoration specialists have to take all kinds of precautions to remove the old paint. Some of those cleaning and removing old paint are protected in what looks like hazmat suits." Candace didn't envy them. She'd donned one of the outfits to inspect and photograph a couple of the horses.

Colin made a face. "That can't be fun. Are you wearing one?"

"Right now I am working on the center tower, where an operator would sit, and the central pole is located in the tower. The paint is badly faded, so I am recreating the original murals on a canvas-type material so the reconstructed tower can be wrapped. There is some debate about how to redo the center tower, as part of it was badly damaged. The only thing anyone agrees on is that it won't be run by an operator sitting inside. Another thing I am glad not to have to deal with."

"Do you like the job?"

"It is different. Much of it is like paint by number since I am repainting what someone already created. In some ways it is strangely satisfying. I feel like the old artist is smiling down on me for carrying on his or her legacy. I have found a few initials that make me think there were several painters." Candace lay back and contemplated the stars. She had always believed in a heaven, but other than her aunt's incessant genealogy stories, she'd never deeply contemplated the lives or stories of people who'd lived before. She pictured someone sitting on a stool with the unpainted animal, trying to decide if lavender was too odd a color for the mane.

Next to her, Colin rolled onto his back. He held her hand again, his fingers exploring her wrist and sending wonderful chills up her arm. Cells that had gone her entire life without being noticed now made their presence known. They lay in silence until a plane crossed the sky, its red lights interrupting the view.

Candace blinked, realizing how close to falling asleep she was. "I think I should get to my place." She searched for a button or lever to return the sofa to a sitting position.

"It is on my side." The seat began to rise. Halfway up it stopped. She turned to find Colin only inches away, studying her. He leaned over and quickly pressed his lips to hers, then leaped back.

"That was terrible, wasn't it?"

What had he done? It certainly wasn't what he'd planned or visualized. The kiss was more like the one between the kids he had seen on a viral video where the little girl had started to cry. Only Candace wasn't crying.

The need to apologize filled him. "I'm sorry. I know I can do better."

She blinked a couple times before sitting up. Colin pushed the button to bring the sofa into a full sitting position. "I studied so much and watched all these moves. Can I—"

Candace placed two fingers on his lips. "A kiss isn't something you can analyze. It is something you feel." She moved her hand over his heart. "Close your eyes and try to clear your brain."

He closed his eyes, but his mind was racing. *What did I do wrong? What should I do now? Try again? Move to a different city?*

"Breathe in through your nose and out through pursed lips." Her fingers rubbed gently across his forehead. "Concentrate on breathing."

Like that was possible with her fingers running across his brow and him knowing he had just delivered the worst kiss in the history of mankind.

Her fingers then trailed down his cheek and along his jaw. One traced his lower lip. "Keep breathing. In. Out."

She was so close her breath brushed his cheek. Her fingers ran back over his brow and into his hair. *In, out. In, out.* Concentrating on his breathing, he let the sensation her fingers were causing wash over him. Then something brushed his lips. A millisecond had passed before he realized Candace was kissing him. Without thinking, he responded, learning and apologizing for his earlier ineptitude at the same time.

She pulled back and placed her forehead against his. "Next time, don't think about it so much."

Next time? She would let him kiss her again. *Again!*

He tilted his head and captured her lips and let himself just feel. He ended the kiss surprised to discover that breathless wasn't only a Hollywood invention.

"I should take you home." He offered Candace his hand and led her back down the spiral staircase.

The elevator definitely needed a slow mode. He didn't kiss her at her door, afraid he might not stop. It wasn't until he was back in the elevator that he thought of another good reason not to kiss her at the door—the hallway cameras. Maybe it was a good thing the elevator had descended so fast. He wasn't tempted to kiss her in there, where other cameras could spy on them.

Hand-holding hadn't been diminished in his estimation. But kissing—well, not his first try—but the others? Now he understood why there were so many songs about it. For the first time in years, Colin fell asleep without counting to one hundred in binary code. *534 days.*

thirteen

CANDACE STEPPED OUT OF THE shower and wrapped a towel around her. The foggy mirror reminded her of the necessity of using the fan. There hadn't been one in Art House, and she was forever forgetting to turn the one in the apartment on. Using a hand towel, she cleared the mirror. Eyebrow-less and hairless, her reflection blinked back at her. For the past week, she had been pondering letting Colin see this side of her. Today would be as good a day as any. October was breast cancer–awareness month. As she did every year, she would wear her pink wigs nearly every other day. This Saturday she would go to the cancer wing of the children's hospital and talk to the teens there. This year she had been asked to give the keynote address at the loss-support group she had helped cofound after her mother had passed away.

THE ONLY REASON SHE HAD agreed to speak on the ten-year anniversary of the group was that she had been sure she would not be around to deliver the speech. Like half the world, Candace had a reasonable fear of public speaking. Fortunately, she didn't get ill or anything, but she did end up running to the bathroom twice as often before a speech than was usual. Which usually wasn't embarrassing unless she got toilet paper stuck to her shoe.

Would Colin come if she invited him? Probably, but was he prepared to see that part of her world? Few people were. Witnessing the bravery of a ten-year-old with terminal cancer or a superhero-cape-clad three-year-old so weakened by chemo that someone had to push them in a wheelchair weren't things that were easy to see. The children loved it when she took off whatever outlandish wig she was wearing and let them play stick the ponytail on her head—a game she'd invented when one of her young friends was having a particularly difficult time adjusting to her own hair loss.

Yes, it was time for Colin to see her head in its natural state. As she dressed, she pondered the how. Just whipping off her wig of the day in the middle of one of their very enjoyable kissing sessions didn't seem like the best idea.

Candace drove to the warehouse without a clue as to how to go about it. Once in the studio, she exchanged her wig for a scarf. Getting paint out of her long pink locks was not worth the risk. Scarfs were so much easier to clean and much cheaper to replace.

Today she worked on a zebra wearing a crown of flowers. The white paint had contained lead, so the refinishers had completely stripped the animal. Only the shorter mane and tail differentiated the zebra from a horse that had once been mostly white.

Rick, the project supervisor, came in shortly before lunch. "Candace, come see what we found. You will need to put on a mask and may want gloves."

She followed him to the other end of the building where most of the heavy sanding and stripping was being done.

"Over here, on the swan."

A worker she didn't immediately recognize due to the full hazmat suit she wore held the head of the swan and stared down into the body. "Marv, I was wrong. I think there are maybe a hundred notes in here."

"It looks like lovers used to stick notes in between the head and the body of the swan. We have only recovered a couple as the paper is fragile, and we wondered if you had any ideas on preserving the notes."

They gathered around a work table where two very wrinkled papers lay. The first was in faded ink.

Dorothy,
I love you forever.
George

The second had been torn, and the pencil scratches were illegible, with the exception of a heart and an arrow.

The woman removed the helmet of her suit. Candace should have guessed it was Sally, one of the master restoration artists, from the red hair. "I think we can photograph them, but we need a better camera. It may be that someone can use some type of photo-manipulation program on them. But they'll need to be treated carefully."

"Do they have much paint residue on them?"

Sally shook her head. "No, the interior of the swan wasn't painted, so I think they are chemical free. The swab test I ran was clean."

Candace studied the notes. "Harmon Media has an archive where they keep copies of all their magazines dating back to the early 1800s. I am sure they have specialists who would know how to handle the papers, and I have an old roommate who does amazing things with digital manipulations."

Rick grunted. "How are we supposed to get in touch with Harmon media? Short of contacting Mr. Gooding, I doubt they will give us the time of day, and if one of those rags writes a story on this and Mr. Gooding doesn't want them to, we will all be jobless."

"One of my old roommates works with Preston Harmon. Let me give her a call." Candace was stretching the term "works with," but she didn't need Rick to know she was friends with

Abbie Harmon. The supervisor was already annoyed she knew Nick Gooding.

"You had better talk to Mr. Gooding first. He might not want the Harmons in his business." Rick glared at her.

Candace pulled the phone out of her pocket. "I'll take a couple of photos and text them with our idea." She snapped the photos and left the room, reasonably sure the real reason Rick had included her in the find was so she would contact Nick directly instead of him having to go through various channels and secretaries.

The photos accompanied a detailed text asking Preston to share the find with Abbie and Mandy.

A half hour later, Nick returned her text with a call. "I just got off the phone with my lawyer, who is going to draw up a nondisclosure. I am not worried about Preston's word, but it is better to give his employees a reason to keep the carousel under wraps for now. He said the head archivist will be thrilled to have something new to do and should be contacting you after lunch. His name is Morry, and he's in his sixties and is slightly deaf from working out on the print floor as a boy. Preston doesn't want Abbie near the warehouse due to the toxins."

Pregnancy and lead didn't mix. Neither did any level of uranium. Mandy was nursing Joy and probably shouldn't be around the notes or warehouse either. So much for including her friends in her project.

"Thanks, Nick. Do you want to see any of the progress?"

"Only if you find a very nicely worded note, maybe something from the past, that will help me with my future."

"They are all love notes." Sappy, wonderful reminders of the nature of love. Hundreds of lovers must have kissed in the swan, each thinking their love would last forever. Candace pondered how many of those notes were the beginning of a wonderful life and which were the beginning of heartbreak.

"I know."

Candace wondered if he was talking about her cousin Zoe. But that kind of prying would get her in trouble. "I'll let you know if I find something super romantic. Although Morry will know more than I will." What would make one super romantic instead of superficial? Perhaps not hiding it in the first place.

"Thanks, Candace. Have a good week." Nick's number disappeared from her screen as the call ended.

Candace found Rick and Sally eating lunch in the break room. Someone had set a plastic pumpkin on one of the tables. Nothing like starting Halloween thirty days early.

Rick set his sandwich down when Candace delivered the news that the archivist would be over soon. "I suppose he will want to tell us how to do things."

"I've never met him, so I have no idea. He may have some ideas about getting the notes out without destroying them."

"We already solved that. The swan's tail is a separate piece. We popped it off and were able to dump all the notes out."

Sally flipped her braid behind her shoulder. "There are probably a couple hundred notes. Can you imagine all those lovers? The swan is up on the second level. I wondered if they tried to steal kisses when the swan was on the back side of the tower." The romantic sigh she let out seemed lost on Rick, who glared at them.

"Back to work, ladies. I'd hate to have our visitor find us sitting around and shooting the breeze."

Candace took a hard candy from the pumpkin as she left the room. Popping it in her mouth, she thought of a way to show Colin her lack of locks.

—**Pumpkin carving my apartment tonight? 7-ish?**

Colin couldn't recall the last time he'd carved a pumpkin—probably with his nanny when he was seven or eight. **Seven is great. Do I need to bring something?**

—Just wear old clothes. It can be messy.

I bet you do cool things with your pumpkin.

—I am a traditionalist, triangle eyes and all, but if you want, we can find some patterns to download.

"Sabrina, find me some Star Wars jack-o-lantern patterns."

"I have found over three hundred patterns. Would you like to refine the search parameters?"

"Sabrina, sort on skill level—easy or novice."

"There are twenty patterns."

"Sabrina, eliminate patterns on the Dark Side."

"Eliminating all patterns printed in black."

"Sabrina, send the twenty easy patterns to the laser printer."

"Confirmed."

Colin turned his attention back to his phone.

Sabrina located some patterns.

—Why am I worried?

You just don't like her because she lives with me.

—She is an AI. However, if you are telling me she is self-aware, that is creepy.

Colin laughed.

I'd have to stop talking to her when I have an idea in the shower.

—TMI. See you tonight.

Colin stared at the screen. What else was he supposed to do when he realized what code he needed to change when he was in the shower? Write on the door with soap? Colin pulled up the app he was working on and tried to concentrate. Maybe he should go into the office more. It was hard to focus when he had a date with Candace to think about.

Soon he was deep into his work. Not even Janie's humming as she dusted around him disturbed him.

Sabrina's voice interrupted him. "It is 6:45. I see from your texts you need to be at Candace's apartment at seven. Please clean up now."

Colin turned off his computer. He had forgotten to set the alarm again. Sabrina was getting better at scanning emails and texts to add appointments to his calendar. He didn't need to change as he already had on a T-shirt that would make his mother yell if she saw it. He didn't see a reason why not to wear the shirts he'd gotten at various computer and sci-fi conventions just because he could buy ridiculously overpriced ones from some shop or another with a fancy name.

He arrived at Candace's apartment a minute before seven. Her pink hair matched her pink tunic and pants. After she closed the door, he leaned down and kissed her hello. After a minute, she pulled back and smiled. "There will be time for that later. Did you bring your patterns?"

Colin produced the papers Sabrina had printed, and Candace flipped through them. "You seem to have a definite theme here. Which one were you planning on doing?"

"The easiest one."

Candace pulled a pattern out of the stack.

"Not a stormtrooper." Colin pulled out a different one.

"The little robot is going to be harder."

"You can help me."

Candace grabbed his hand and led him into the kitchen. "Choose a pumpkin. I'm going to switch for a scarf. I like pumpkin spice but not on my wigs."

Colin watched her retreat into the bedroom. She didn't need to wear a scarf for his sake. Someday she wouldn't feel the need. It wasn't like he didn't know she was bald. She returned predictably in a pink scarf.

"What is up with all the pink?"

"Cancer-awareness month."

"Your mom died of breast cancer, didn't she?"

Candace nodded as she spread several pages from the *Tribune* over the table. "I tend to go a bit overboard trying to remind all my friends to self-check for cancer."

"Nick says we all need a cause. I just haven't found one yet."

"Nick has enough causes for everyone. Isn't his father the philanthropist of the year again?"

Colin shrugged. He never paid attention to stuff like that. Although the Goodings seemed to be just that, so many in the ten-digit club just tried to out do each other with their charitable giving.

"Speaking of causes, I have some things this weekend in Indianapolis that deal with childhood cancer and an address at a cancer-loss support group I helped start. Would you like to come?"

"Are you asking me to go away with you for the weekend?"

She blushed. He loved to tease her just so he could see the pink in her cheeks. "Not exactly. You do have to get your own room and everything."

"I'd love to come." Colin finished with the lid of his jack-o-lantern and pulled it off.

Candace did the same with hers and started scooping the slimy pumpkin guts into a bowl. "Oh, rats. I got it on my scarf." She went over to the sink and rinsed her hands before taking off the scarf and rinsing it.

Colin tried not to stare. She looked just like he imagined, only prettier. He double-checked his hands for pumpkin slime before joining her at the sink. He reached over her shoulder and turned off the water. With one hand, he turned Candace toward him. With the other, he traced where her hairline should be, from the top of her head to her ear. Then he kissed the top of her head, his kisses following the same trail his fingers had. "Thank you." His voice came out all husky and odd.

Candace tipped her head up, and he could see there was a tear at the corner of her eye. "No. Thank *you*." She captured his lips with hers.

He tasted tears and pulled back, running one hand over her smooth head. "Why are you crying? Did I do something wrong?"

She swiped a tear from her cheek. "Nothing is wrong. I just wasn't sure how you would react. I thought you might be sickened."

"Why would you think that?"

"My father can't stand seeing me without my wigs. He has a hard time with the scarf. So I worried that even though you seem to really like me that—"

What was inside him went beyond like, but he wasn't sure how to say it. "You not having a wig on doesn't change things for me. Well, actually it does. It makes things better. I am honored you would let me see you this way."

She snuggled into his shoulder, and he held her, resting his cheek on top of her head. After several minutes, Candace stepped back. "It makes things better?"

"It is like you have let me into this secret part of you. It isn't a secret that you are bald. But you never really relax when you are in a wig. Especially one that itches like the one you had on the other night at the symphony."

"You noticed?"

"I hoped you would take it off in the car on the way home so you could get some relief."

"Is that why you were so careful not to touch it when we kissed?"

"I didn't know if it would make it worse. Next time when your hair is bothering you, just take it off."

"I will." Candace reached for his hand. "We'd better finish these pumpkins."

She didn't put on a scarf the rest of the night. They put the pumpkins out on her deck, where they would stay cold and hopefully not rot.

After they cleaned up, they sat on the couch.

"I'm so glad my baldness didn't put you off. You know, if you come with me you will see little kids, four-year-olds and even younger, whose heads resemble mine. I take my wig off a lot, especially when talking with the teen girls. They tend to feel the loss of their hair more keenly than the other children."

Colin rubbed his hand over his own hair. "Should I shave mine?"

"No. You are not a survivor. It will be more impressive that I can introduce you as my boyfriend. When you look at me that way, it will make all the girls giggle."

What am I doing wrong now? "Look at you how?"

"Like you want me to shut up so you can kiss me silly."

Colin had no clue how she knew that was precisely what he wanted to do, but since she didn't seem averse to the idea, he kissed her. A thought stopped him. "Am I really your boyfriend?"

"You had better be. I don't kiss acquaintances like this." She pulled him into another kiss.

Boyfriend. That meant she was his girlfriend? He thought of stopping and asking if he was right, but that would mean stopping the sensations running through his body at rates he couldn't comprehend. Besides, he was pretty sure her kiss was the answer to his unasked question.

fourteen

THE DAY IN THE CANCER ward was more difficult than ever. Candace tried to come up with a reason she felt that way. Some of the patients she'd met before were back after a relapse. It wasn't the first time she met some who probably would go home only to require hospice care, if they made it home at all. The mothers wore their usual brave smiles. Most likely they watered their pillows at night. The youngest patients wore yarn wigs fancy enough to make Rapunzel jealous or capes finer than Superman's.

AS USUAL, SHE CHEATED AT the game of pin the ponytail on Candace to avoid getting poked in the eye. Colin knelt by child after child and talked to each one, drawing out their wishes and dreams. His phone version of Sabrina told jokes and offered absurdly wrong facts. One little boy argued with the AI over the number of states in the US with other children joining in. It wasn't until they were in the car headed back to the hotel that Candace realized Sabrina had recorded all the wishes and dreams of the children.

"I know some organizations help with some of these wishes, like trips to amusement parks and things, but do you think there is anything I could do?" asked Colin as he scrolled through his phone.

"I'm sure you could make a hefty donation or two."

"That isn't enough. Like eight-year-old Peter wants his mommy to live in a house again. Apparently they ended up selling it to pay for their part of his treatments."

"Sometimes that happens. My father ended up selling our farm to my uncle, Zoe's father, to help pay for my mother's and my treatments. The chemo drug that worked for me wasn't approved by our insurance. Of course, it had the side effect of never needing to purchase shampoo again."

"So, do you think I could do something?"

"Why not? You have the resources." Candace couldn't help but think of the things she would do if she could literally spend millions without thinking about it.

"What about the carousel and theme park you envisioned?"

"That is a massive project. It may take Nick's and Daniel's involvement as well, maybe even Preston's and Kyle's. An indoor, climate-controlled park that would need to be as clean as a hospital room isn't a small project." More like pie-in-the-sky massive. The cleaning costs alone would be prohibitive, not to mention the fact that it would earn zero revenue.

"I have been thinking about the merry-go-round. Isn't that going to be almost impossible to clean?"

"I've been looking at a few different sealants and coatings. Some polyurethane products look quite promising, but I really don't know as much as I should." Candace was getting to the point she had exhausted her online knowledge base. Sally was a helpful resource, but Rick had found problems with the concept at every turn.

"Hmmm. I am a dunce when it comes to chemistry, but it seems like there should be some coatings that would be what you need."

"We don't need to solve it today. I don't think the carousel is even 10 percent done. I already asked my old professor, Dr. Christensen, to find me a couple of interns for the spring semester. The foundation painting goes pretty fast, but the details will take much longer to finish. It's hard to believe everything was hand carved or, in the case of all the iron, forged by hand. The flowers I have been painting on the zebra's head are so detailed." Rick had caught her using dental tools to scrape out a few of the paint flecks they'd missed in the petals yesterday. He felt that the job his crew had completed was adequate. Candace wanted amazing, not adequate. Yes, when she was done painting, no one would know, but *she* would, and that made a difference.

The driver pulled up to the hotel. Andrew, who was the only bodyguard besides the driver for this trip, got out first. Candace was glad Jethro Hastings agreed that the hospital visit required minimum security. It meant fewer people around—a win for the children and for her. As of yet, no one had seen the need to give her personal security. The irony that Colin was the wealthiest of the six billionaires she knew and the least known kept things simple. His introverted lifestyle kept him out of the camera's eye. Mandy speculated that not one in fifteen paparazzi even knew what Colin looked like as he appeared publicly with Daniel only on the rarest of occasions.

The driver got the door. Colin escorted her up to her suite, which he had upgraded from the room she had across town in a well-known chain hotel. His reasoning was if he had to stay in a hotel with better security, she had to as well.

"What do you want to do for dinner?" he asked.

"I need to go over my notes for my speech tomorrow. I was thinking of just ordering room service. I know that isn't much fun for you."

"I don't mind. I could come and keep you company?" The sentence ended with a hopeful question mark.

Candace bit her lip. She wasn't ready to share what she planned on saying or wanted to highlight for the support group tomorrow. If Colin was in the room while she prepared, there would be thoughts she couldn't express, and he would hold her if she cried. Normally that would be a good thing as it would end the tears. Tonight, she needed to feel. "I need to finish writing this alone. I am afraid you are a huge distraction."

"I understand." His pinched brow told her he didn't.

She kissed him softly before opening the door to her suite. "I'll call you when I am done. Maybe we can watch an episode of some old sitcom." Candace closed the door before she was tempted to let him in. Part of the problem she had with tomorrow's address was separating her mother's pain from her own. Few of the fifteen chapters' support-group members had firsthand experience with what their lost loved one had faced. Candace intimately knew it all—from the disbelief at the diagnosis to the putting your life in the hands of a world-renowned surgeon you only got to talk with for ten minutes. How could she convey those feelings she needed to?

She paced the room, wondering what to disclose. Who could she ask for advice? Candace scrolled through her contact list. Odd—she didn't even recall putting that number in. She hit the green icon and waited while it rang.

"Hello, Reverend Cavanagh? This is Candace. We met at Sean and Tessa's wedding."

A quiet evening had never bothered Colin before, but tonight his mind jumped from one project to another. Peter and his wish for a house wouldn't leave him alone. It only took him a few minutes to discover where Peter had lived before his diagnosis. It helped that the boy had described everything from the basketball hoop to the name of his next-door neighbor's cat. The house was not for sale, of course. However, there were four or five comparable homes in the area. Other than his father's passing, Colin didn't have much experience with death. What would Peter's parents and sister want other than to have Peter well? He couldn't give them that, but he could provide Peter his wish. He found the number for Peter's mother on her social media account. It went to voicemail. Colin didn't leave a message as he realized that this might be something the lawyers needed to be involved in. He made a note and moved to the next child's wish.

She wanted her baby sister to remember her. A video camera and some dress-up clothes could easily make that wish a reality. Colin continued going through the wishes. Some, like a real pet unicorn, were not possible with any amount of money. Others were simple. His favorite was from a thirteen-year-old girl who wanted to give her mom a locket with her photo in it from when she still had hair. "I want her to remember the times before the hard stuff. Like when I threw a tantrum because she bought the wrong color of socks. I want her to remember me as a normal teen."

Just before midnight, his phone rang with Candace's song. "Hey, are you done?"

"Yes, but I am pretty drained." Her voice sounded as if she had been crying.

"Shall I come over?"

"I'm not sure it's wise."

"Why not?"

"You know those dating lines we discussed? I'm feeling…well, let's just say I won't want to let you go."

Colin cleared his throat. Candace had very clear boundaries, ones she never crossed. "What if I set my phone alarm for a half hour? I won't cross any lines."

"Forty-five minutes?"

He had his limits too, but he didn't know if he could be the strong one for more than a half hour. "A half hour. You need sleep."

"Okay."

She opened the door before he knocked and launched herself into his arms. Colin held her with one arm as he closed the door. "What is wrong?"

"I ended up calling my dad and sister. Part of the reason I started these groups is we couldn't talk about Mom or about me. In some ways, we still can't. I asked Dad why he doesn't like to see my head."

"What did he say?"

"He says he thinks it means he failed me. The drug had a flaw, and he blames himself. The drug may have saved my life, yet he blames himself." She shook her head, trying to wrap her mind around his guilt. "We talked about my hair and a few of the things Reverend Cavanagh told me."

"When did you talk to the reverend?"

"I called him earlier this evening. He asked me why I'd created the group, and I told him I hoped it would help us talk. Apparently, I have helped hundreds of others talk, just not my family. He suggested I call Dad and my sister. I nearly hung up on him, but the reverend is persuasive. In the end, I am glad I talked to my dad. I told him about you and your reaction to my bald head. He wants to meet you."

"Really?" Meeting the parents was a big thing, right? He didn't know if he was ready or what he would say to Candace's dad. *Your daughter is amazing, by the way. I had a friend make up this job just so she could be near me. Oh, and if she agrees, I want to marry her. I've been watching proposal scenes on the Hearthfire channel all month.*

"I told dad about my ten-year plan. He told me he never heard a single doctor give me a so-long-to-live timeline like they gave my mom. Her cancer was already very advanced when they found it. When they found mine I was only at stage two. Dad told me about one of Mom's surgeries that she really didn't need as she knew it wouldn't prolong her life. She just did it to make mine easier for me. I wish he would have told me before now. I can't believe she went through all that pain just so she could support me." Candace produced a tissue from her pocket and turned away as she blew her nose. "Sorry. I'm a big snotty mess."

Colin handed her a pocket handkerchief. "These absorb more."

"You even carry a handkerchief in your jeans?"

"Mom insisted. I never broke the habit." Actually, it was very convenient for all sorts of things. Janie couldn't wash off the notes he scribbled on them in permanent marker, although he rarely did that anymore. A tablet didn't ever get tossed in the laundry basket.

Candace wiped her eyes and took a deep breath.

"How did your talk with your sister go?" Colin realized he had never even heard Candace say her sister's name.

Candace started pacing. "The same as always. I think she's spent the last ten years in denial. She is still angry at me for ruining her senior year of high school. It isn't my fault I got more attention than she did. She claims I got all this time with mom that she didn't. Mom and I took chemo treatments together. We had surgeries in the same hospital to remove tumors. Mom and I shared the pain, and she is jealous! I don't understand. She is the one who went to her high school graduation and has her white picket fence and two practically perfect children and a husband who adores her. She got everything she planned on, but she still blames me. I don't get it."

"I could be wrong, but it sounds like you are jealous of her too." The words slipped out before he could stop them.

Candace spun to face him, her hands on her hips.

Colin held up his hands. "She has a perfectly normal, somewhat pedestrian lifestyle. That is what you once wanted too, isn't it?"

Her hands slid from her hips. "Once upon a time ago I did. But those dreams are gone."

The next question sat on his tongue. He didn't have the courage to ask whether she still wanted a husband and children.

Sabrina's voice interrupted his thoughts. "Time is up. Your time is up. Go home."

"She has incredibly bad timing." Candace stuck her tongue out at his phone. "But thank you for listening."

"We can save the kissing for another night." Colin drew her close for one good-night kiss.

Before he could start the second one, Sabrina interrupted again. "Your time is up."

Candace started giggling. "Night, Colin."

Colin returned to his room and vowed that next time he would set a standard alarm.

fifteen

"I COFOUNDED THIS ORGANIZATION IN hopes of bringing my own family healing after my mother's death from cancer. But I never fully took advantage of the services. Why? Because talking can be as painful as surgery and as scary as chemotherapy. But if we don't communicate our feelings and thoughts, the silence grows into a malignancy that can't be cut out by surgeons or shrunken by drugs. Last night I spoke with a wise man who urged me to end the silence in my own family by saying what no one wanted to hear. A simple phone call healed years of miscommunication with my father. Things were said that brought us closer and ended the silence."

"There are many things we can't control in life, like whether or not the cancer will spread, but we can control our communications and keep them from devolving into the cancer of silence. I urge each of you not to allow your silence to grow until it is terminal. Thank you."

Judging by the applause, the speech went well. Colin stood at the back of the room next to Andrew, who clapped too. Since he was there, she kept the references to her own cancer minimal.

There was another silence she needed to face. Reverend Cavanagh had asked her about her next ten-year plan. She had ideas, but until she could tell Colin everything, she couldn't move forward either.

There was no privacy on the short flight back to Chicago.

Nor was there any during dinner with Mandy, Daniel, Abbie, and Preston. They ended up watching a movie with the other couples, and Candace didn't want to talk in front of the driver.

Sunday, Colin left with Daniel on a business trip to Hong Kong. Candace tried to write her thoughts in an email.

Twice.

She ended up just texting generic what's-up messages.

The silence started to grow.

The familiar lights of the Chicago skyline filled Colin's window. O'Hare never looked so good. Daniel's complaining about being away from Mandy on these trips made more sense now. China was especially tricky as Colin always felt like someone was watching him. Perhaps he had seen one too many spy movies. Or maybe there was something else. The two brief phone conversations he had with Candace seemed off. But then, either he was ready for bed or she was. And she was still in yesterday when he was in today.

He couldn't wait to see her, but then he could. Candace's father was visiting. Maybe it was his own unease at meeting him that caused Colin to think something was off. Next to him, Daniel stretched. "Please tell me we never have to fly again."

"You know, we could just get a corporate jet like Preston's."

"We have one."

Colin sat up. "We do?"

"Yes, but it is impractical to take to Hong Kong, though I took it to London in July."

"Why don't I know these things?"

"Probably because you don't pay attention in all those meetings we have. We also have a smaller one. You have flown in it several times."

"I knew about that one. Which one did we take to New York for the wedding?"

"Preston's. His is a family jet, so no red tape for vacations."

Colin stowed his tablet. "Maybe I should get a private one."

"It depends. Will you fly it more than you do your red car?"

"Of course. I'll have a pilot."

Daniel laughed. "That car is so wasted on you."

Colin smiled. He knew his red car, a Lamborghini, would have been well loved in many a garage. It was the last gift he'd received from his father, so he'd held on to it even if driving wasn't something he enjoyed.

Which made his chauffeured ride back to the penthouse all the better. He could text while someone else drove.

Heading home from O'Hare.

—I made dinner. It will be ready in thirty. Ready to meet my dad?

Was anybody ever ready to meet the man he hoped to make his father-in-law?

Looking forward to it.

Colin headed for the penthouse first for a change of clothing and to splash water on his face. His body had no idea what time zone he was in. He asked Sabrina twice, but the answer made no sense to him. The only thing he could hear clearly was his bed. All he needed was some sleep to make the world right. Well, sleep and Candace. Since the two needs were mutually exclusive at the moment, he took the elevator down ten floors and knocked on Candace's door.

He needs sleep. Candace gave Colin a peck on the cheek. With her father in the next room, she didn't dare go for a real kiss. "Come on in and meet my dad." She took him by the arm and led him into the living area, where her father stood from the couch.

"Dad, this is Colin. Colin, my dad."

Her father extended his hand. "Neil Wilson. Nice to meet you."

Colin shook her father's hand and yawned. "Sorry, I'm thirteen hours ahead or eleven behind."

"Don't worry about it. Candace told me you would be a little jet lagged. I take it she underestimated how much."

A buzzer in the kitchen rang. Candace ran to pull out the lasagna, worried about leaving the two men alone. She set the lasagna on the table, added ice to the water glasses, and set out the salad. When she returned to the living area, Colin was snoring softly.

Dad smiled a bemused smile. "I'll give him points for meeting me."

"I don't think you should take it personally." Poor Colin. He'd tried so hard.

"Dinner can wait a few moments. Why don't you wake him up enough to get him back up to his apartment?"

Candace crouched in front of her sleeping boyfriend. "Colin?" She shook him gently.

"Huh? Wa—? I'm awake." He rubbed his eyes.

"Not really. Let's get you up to your place, and you can see me tomorrow."

Colin nodded and stood, swaying a bit.

Dad stood in the kitchen doorway. "Perhaps you'd better escort him up. I don't want him riding the elevator all night."

Candace wrapped an arm around Colin and headed for the elevator.

The lights flickered on when they entered Colin's apartment. "Welcome, Candace. Welcome, Colin."

Candace ignored the AI and walked Colin to his bedroom. The door was locked.

"Sabrina, open Colin's bedroom door."

"I am sorry. The bedroom doors are to remain locked when Candace Wilson is in the apartment."

Really? Do you think I am going to take advantage of him? Candace kept the thought to herself.

Colin muttered something, but the AI didn't respond. Candace steered him to the big couch in the entertainment room. "Sorry, you'll have to nap here until I am gone. Hopefully Janie will come soon."

He wrapped his arms around her much the way a zombie would in a B movie. "Don't go."

Candace extricated herself and covered Colin with a throw blanket. "I need to. My dad is waiting." She placed a kiss on his forehead and turned down the light. Even if she did stay with him, he wouldn't remember anything in the morning.

The elevator wouldn't open.

"Sabrina, please call the elevator."

"Sorry, he said don't go. You must stay."

"Sabrina, he is talking in his sleep. Please let me go."

"Orders do not compute."

Candace went back into the room were Colin slept. "Colin, please wake up. Your AI won't let me leave."

"What?"

"Please tell Sabrina I can go home."

He blinked a couple of times. "Sabrina, Candace is going home. Start evening lockdown procedures after she leaves."

"Thank you." Candace kissed him on the cheek before hurrying to the elevator, half afraid Sabrina would start her evening lockdown before she could escape. This time the elevator opened. She pushed the button for her floor, but the elevator didn't move. "Sabrina, please let me go to my floor."

The elevator closed. Candace rubbed her head. The lasagna was probably cold, and what father would believe her boyfriend's AI had held her hostage?

sixteen

TWO DAYS LATER, COLIN WAS fully cognizant of his surroundings. "Sabrina, what day is it?"

"Wednesday, 7:10 a.m."

Make that three days. How did Daniel do it? The three or four times a year Colin traveled more than three time zones messed him up for days. He called Candace. "Good morning."

"Are you back among the living?"

"I think so. What did I miss?" Janie had woken him a couple times and forced food into him. Sabrina spoke random things that made him wish he had one of the old alarm clocks that turned off when it was hit.

"You have talked to me on the phone three times, but I don't think you were awake."

He rubbed his forehead, trying to remember the calls. "I hope I didn't say anything too stupid. I don't remember. I think I met your dad. And I dreamed Sabrina held you hostage."

"Both of those things happened. I hope she isn't listening to you now. She may get ideas."

"I can't believe she did that." What had he misprogrammed now? And meeting her father, that probably hadn't gone well. Maybe it was best he didn't remember.

Something scraped on the other end of the line. "I think she listens to you more than you know."

"Can we do something tonight? Dinner and a movie?"

"Sure. I'm in the parking garage, and my hands-free is on the fritz. Can we finish catching up later?"

Colin nodded, then remembered to speak. "See you tonight."

By lunchtime, Candace had made up her mind. Tonight she would tell Colin everything he would need to know. Before she lost her nerve, she texted.

How about we just order in and see a movie on streaming?

—Sounds good. I haven't had a minute to plan. Went to the office, and Daniel is making me work.

Poor boy. Reading documents or something else that doesn't involve a computer.

—Ha ha. You know me so well. Text me when you get home.

Will do. Chinese or Italian?

—Not oriental, please.

LOL

Candace finished her lunch and wished she could text Zoe for some extra strength. But Zoe wasn't allowed phones during work hours. She hadn't talked over the need to tell Colin about the extent of her cancer during his weekend visit. Her new-found openness with her dad didn't extend that far yet. However, it did extend far enough for her father to begin to mediate between her and Crystal. Apparently Crystal's life wasn't as perfect as Candace had believed. Her nephew was on the autism spectrum, something Crystal had never divulged during their few phone calls a year. They started to plan Thanksgiving dinner together.

For a split second, she considered asking Crystal's advice. But they had never discussed the outcome of her surgeries before.

Candace changed her focus to the lavender horse she was working on. Fortunately, nothing was challenging about the day's painting.

By the time she drove back to the apartment building, Candace was worried her nerves would spin out of control and she would blurt everything out at once.

Candace was wearing his favorite wig and carrying takeout burger bags. He could kiss her already. Sometime during the second meeting of the afternoon, he realized they hadn't kissed for a week and a half. He didn't count the kisses Candace had given him when he'd gotten back Sunday or Monday. Even though he technically knew it was Sunday, his brain still said Monday. "Good old American. Bless you, my friend."

"If I knew this was all you needed to be happy, I would have brought them to you two days ago. Actually, I did try to come up, but Sabrina wouldn't let me out of the elevator."

Colin wondered what order he had given the AI to produce that action. At some point, his housekeeper had been allowed in. "So, first Sabrina won't let you leave, then she won't let you in?"

Candace set the bags on the table and sorted the contents. "No offense, but I think she has a few flaws. I've always felt that computers and I were not very compatible, but now I know it." Her teasing smile let him know it wasn't a problem, yet.

"I must have been distracted when I worked on her code last time."

"I didn't think you got distracted when you were thinking about code."

He felt the blood rush to his face. He hadn't gotten distracted before, but now that he was holding hands and kissing and entertaining daydreams of marriage to Candace, he was majorly distracted. Hopefully, when things were not so new, he'd be able to focus. Many married men, as well as men in committed relationships, managed to function in their day-to-day lives. When he got his first smartphone, he had been the same way until he'd learned every nuance of the device. Relationships must be the same way. Candace waited for his answer. "You, us, kissing."

She dipped her head and hid behind the locks of her wig. When she looked back up, she was blushing too. "I can see how that could be distracting."

"Did you realize it has been over 250 hours since we last kissed? Real kisses, not those quick pecks when I got back. And that is real consecutive hours, not me being in Hong Kong all mixed up."

Candace covered her mouth, then took a sip of her drink. "I was thinking more than ten days, but not in terms of hours. Are you trying to say you missed me?"

He set down his food. "Ya, I did. I was never homesick, even when I was ten and got sent off to school. I didn't want to be there, but I didn't want to be home either. This was the first time I wanted to come home—here, to you." Talking to Candace loosened all his filters, but he didn't care. Other than Daniel and a little with Nick, he never shared many of his thoughts. Never wanted to.

Candace stood and cleared her garbage away. Colin did the same. "What movie do you want to see?"

She folded her arms and leaned against the counter. "I'm not sure it will matter. You seem to have other things on your mind."

He rubbed his forehead. "I am trying to be a gentleman and control myself around you, even if I am blurting out everything I am thinking."

"Everything?" She stretched her hand to reach his and pushed off the counter.

No, not everything. He still needed to say the *L* word, then the *M* word. Good thing they were in alphabetical order. They entered the entertainment room.

"Sabrina, please turn on the Hearthfire streaming channel and locate selections we have not seen."

seventeen

ABSENCE DID MAKE THE HEART grow fonder—or at least it made the hormones build up. Honestly, by the time he did make a move to kiss her, she was ready to take matters into her own hands. His kiss was more pensive and unsure than she recalled from their last kiss. She shifted positions on the couch, swinging her legs across his lap, bringing them closer. Colin paused, then moved his arms behind her back, pulling her even closer, his inexperience with women making the moment all the more dear. Candace wished for a moment she had never made the stupid bucket-list item, but at sixteen she hadn't understood the subtler points of relationships or the depth of feelings that could exist between a man and a woman. She'd only thought of dying without ever being kissed. But being kissed by the right man at the right time was so different than being kissed by someone who just wanted to kiss the cancer girl. This was the type of kiss that had sent all her old roommates to the altar. If only her story could end there. If it could be more than just this moment, this kiss. A tear formed near the corner of her eye, and she was helpless to catch it as Colin rained a row of kisses along her jawline. He stopped and ran his thumb across her cheek. "Are you crying? Did I do something wrong?"

The light from the flickering television reflected in his eyes. Candace hoped he could see hers as she tried to reassure him. "No, you are doing things just right. It's me. Wishing I'd never put kissing guys on that list because this kiss is honestly the best of my life."

His thumb rubbed across her bottom lip. "If you hadn't experienced their kisses, how would you know this was the best?" He smiled big enough that his dimple showed, as if he were pleased by the thought his kisses moved her.

Candace kissed the dimple, not willing to explain or examine the rest of her thoughts. Colin responded with kisses of his own. She allowed her fingers to explore the hair at the nape of his neck as his hand rubbed her back. As their kisses grew deeper, Candace knew she should end the night and go home. There was no place to move forward from here. The dead end this road led to loomed before her. Just one more kiss, one more touch.

He trailed kisses up to her ear. "I love you." His voice was husky. His lips found hers again. Colin's hands moved to her sides, his thumbs caressing her ribs and moving upward.

Danger!

"Stop!" Candace pushed his hands away.

Colin blinked at her, confusion marring his brow.

"I need to go." Candace untangled herself from him and stood to look for her shoes.

He stood beside her, running his hand through his hair. "I'm sorry I got carried away. I didn't—"

Candace shook her head but didn't turn to look at him. "No, Colin. *We* got carried away. But I can't. I never can."

"I didn't mean to cross the line. I know you're not that type—"

She spun around, frustration filling all the places that moments ago had tingled with another emotion. "No! It isn't that I was going to tell you before. I should have. I'm hardly a woman at all. It's all fake!" She pulled off her wig. "The cancer stole it all! I'm not that type of woman because I am barely a woman."

"Candace, you know I don't care about the hair. I love you the way you are." He took a step forward, his arms open.

"Stop!" She took two steps backward. "You don't know who I am." She reached into her shirt with her right hand and pulled out her left prosthesis, then did the same with the other. She held them out to him, cradled in her palms. "A real woman can't do this."

Colin stared at her hands, his jaw working but nothing coming out of his mouth.

Candace dropped the prosthetics on the coffee table next to her wig and ran for the elevator.

Sabrina didn't stop her. Neither did Colin.

"Sabru, Sabrina, ligh—" Colin choked back his emotions and tried again. "Sabrina, lights on."

The living room lights came on. "Shall I turn off the entertainment system?" asked the computerized voice.

"Yes."

Colin sat down and pulled the coffee table over to him. The pieces started to fall into place. Candace's mother had died from breast cancer. They had been in the hospital together. The ten-year plan wasn't like his ten-year plan. It had been all she'd planned.

He dialed Candace's number. Her phone rang from between the couch cushions. He dug it out.

"Sabrina, is Candace in her apartment?"

"I cannot answer. It is against my privacy protocols."

"Sabrina, is Candace in the building?"

"I cannot answer. It is against my privacy protocols."

"Sabrina, is Candace safe?"

"I cannot answer. It is against my privacy protocols."

Colin wanted to hit the computer housing Sabrina's electronic brain.

"Sabrina, override authorization 911. Is there a human in apartment 10B?"

"Password, please."

"Unicorn hair."

"The door was accessed five minutes ago via the keypad. There is one heat signature in the apartment."

"Sabrina. Please alert me if the door to 10B opens."

"I cannot answer. It is against my privacy protocols."

Colin buried his head in his hands. How should he go after her, and what should he say?

"Sabrina, what time is it?"

"12:11 a.m., Thursday, October—"

He cut the computer off before she started with the weather. "Sabrina, email me a memo to fix your time protocol."

His phone pinged with the new email.

Colin gathered Candace's wig and—he wasn't sure what to call them—headed to the elevator. He assumed she would want her phone. The prosthetics weighed more than he thought. Candace probably would not want him carrying them in his hands, so he set them back on the coffee table and went in search of a box or bag. Every single bag he could find came from an electronics or computer store. All of his boxes were the same. He found a shirt box in his closet, complete with the shirt. He took the shirt out but left the tissue paper.

He rearranged the items a couple times before closing the lid and heading down the elevator.

eighteen

CANDACE CLOSED THE DOOR AND sunk to the floor. Tears streamed down her face. What had she done? She had never meant to tell him like that. Just to explain. Outside her family and the doctors, there wasn't a single man who knew. Of her roommates, only Mandy had full knowledge of the extent of the cancer and repercussions. It was too late to call Mandy. Joy had just started sleeping through the night. Zoe—she could call her, but it was an hour later in New York. Candace went to pull out her phone, but it wasn't in her pocket.

SHE COULDN'T FACE HIM AGAIN. No way. She would just have to get a new phone. First she needed to get off the floor.

One deep breath was not enough to give her the strength to move.

Neither were two.

There was a tap on the door above her head.

"Candace?"

Colin. She pushed up with her legs, sliding her back up the door, then turned and leaned her head on the door.

Tap. Tap. "Candace, is that you?"

She turned and leaned against the door. "Yes."

"Will you open the door?"

"I can't." Her voice squeaked out.

"Candace, please?"

She could picture him leaning on the door the same way she was. A sob rose from her throat. "I, I—"

The light thump on the door could have been his forehead. "I have your phone and—" There was a long silence. "I'll leave your things here. Just call me when you are ready."

Candace tried to answer, but her voice wouldn't work.

"Are you still there? Tap twice if you hear me."

She raised her hand. Tap. Tap. Tap. The same three taps her mother had used when she was too weak to talk. *One, two, three— I love you.*

"Night, Candace."

She waited until she heard the ping of the elevator. She expected to see a pile of things on the floor or inside a plastic computer-store bag, not a box taped closed with blue electrical tape. Sitting down on the couch, she opened the box. A note lay on top of the tissue paper. Candace set it aside and checked under the tissue. Her wig lay on top of her prosthetics, which had been nestled into opposite corners of the box inside two of his monogrammed handkerchiefs. More tears escaped as she realized he'd treated them with more care than when she tossed them on his table. Her phone was taped to the center of the box. Of course he wasn't going to let anything happen to her electronics.

The note waited to be read. She unfolded it.

Dearest Candace-
I meant what I said. Call me when you are ready.
Love,
* Colin*

What had he said? Candace replayed the conversation in her head. Her hair—he thought she had been upset over that. She closed her eyes and rubbed her temples, trying to hear the words again.

I love you the way you are.
But that was before he knew she was only part of a woman.
Candace curled up in a ball on her couch.
She'd never be ready to tell him the rest.

For the gazillionth time, Colin asked Sabrina the time. He knew it had to be his imagination, but the AI sounded exasperated. He'd spent the last hour clearing out any glitches in the code, worried he had figured out how to make the AI self-aware. He hadn't. The hour before that, Colin had surfed the statistics of breast-cancer survivors. Breast cancer in teen girls was rare. However, the genetic component would have been a factor. Colin ran some numbers. A teen girl had almost the same chance of getting breast cancer as Sean Cavanagh discovering he was a billionaire. No wonder she had assumed the doctor was talking about her in ten years.

While looking for blogs from survivors, he found a gallery of black-and-white art photos of women who'd had single or double mastectomies. He wouldn't lie—during his lifetime he'd wondered what a female breast felt like. There was more than enough locker room talk that even he had heard some of it. But it wasn't Candace's silhouette that had drawn him to her. After looking at the photos of the survivors, he saw the scars as badges of courage and honor. She could never nurse their children, which, considering how red he turned every time he realized Mandy was feeding Joy, could be a good thing.

A couple of the medical websites indicated there was a chance the chemo had damaged her ovaries and any children would need to come via adoption. He was okay with that, too. Candace was the only woman he'd ever kissed, the only one he ever wanted to kiss. Her prosthetics, he'd learned that term also, did not need to stand in the way of a relationship.

His alarm went off, followed by Sabrina's voice. "Wake up. It is Thursday. You have a meeting with your lawyer at nine thirty to discuss options for helping Peter get a house for his family and other wishes. Daniel is expecting you at noon for lunch with the CEO of a software company you are thinking of acquiring. There are four other deadlines or meetings on your agenda today."

"Sabrina, is Candace still in her apartment?"

"I cannot answer. It is against my privacy protocols."

Colin wanted to toss his ethics out the window. He could get into the building's security system and find out for himself in a matter of minutes. But he had learned his lessons from hacking the Department of Defense. Just because one could didn't mean one should.

He texted instead.

Good morning. I know we need to talk. Can I see you tonight?

He didn't expect an answer right away.

But as the day went on and he still hadn't heard from her, the silence grew more painful.

It was afternoon before Candace dragged herself into the shower. She'd woken up earlier only long enough to text Rick that she was taking a sick day.

Over the last ten years she had gotten good at ignoring the scars. Today she couldn't. Her fingers traced them over and over as her tears mingled with the water from the shower. The agonizing choices she'd made a decade ago came rushing back now. It was possible she could have survived with a lumpectomy of the right breast, but the genetic component of her cancer and the belief that she only had ten years to live had prompted her to take the more radical route—the one her mother had joined her in, although for her mother it was already too late for the mastectomies to prevent further damage. Her cancer had spread to her lymph nodes, bones, and left lung before it was discovered. A discovery that had saved Candace's life as Mom had insisted both her daughters be checked for cancer.

The second mastectomy had been voluntary. At the time it hadn't seemed important to save one of them for future use. It hadn't mattered with the guys she had kissed to fill her bucket list either. Now that she dared to start planning a future that wasn't so finite, she found it mattered after all. She'd read enough books and seen enough movies to know that to most men, breasts were an essential part of relations. She'd never worried about it. She was never going to get married. Never wanted more than a few kisses and a week or two of fun.

The shower grew cold. Candace had questions. As she pulled on her robe and reached for her phone to call Mandy, her eye fell on Crystal's number. Perhaps her sister would be a better choice for this talk.

"Hey, what are you doing, sis?"

"Laundry. It never ends."

"Do you have time for a few questions?"

There was a pause before her sister answered. "Sure. Let me put on some earphones so I can keep folding this stuff."

Candace waited for the click indicating the switch before continuing. "If you don't want to answer anything, that is okay. My first question is, do you think a guy could ever love me?"

"Of course. What isn't to love?"

"Double mastectomy."

"Oh, that. You mean you have never found out?"

"Um, no. You know how Mom felt about premarital relations. I must have gotten that lecture a million times."

"That was probably my fault."

"What do you mean?"

There was a long silence. "I wasn't exactly chaste in high school. Haven't you ever done the math? Your nephew wasn't a preemie."

"I didn't think about it at the time. I was just so jealous you were planning a future with a husband who loved you."

"I was jealous of you getting to finish college and going to exotic places while I was stuck changing diapers and worried that Grant would leave me when he saw the stretch marks."

Candace curled up in her favorite chair. "Did he still love you with stretch marks?"

"We had three miscarriages and another baby, so they didn't stop him.

"You had miscarriages?"

"Yes, but that isn't why you called. We can save that conversation. My answer is I think the right man will probably love you even more because of your scars. There is more to relations than just the physical. There are emotional and spiritual components. When you have the emotional/spiritual link, it is so much better. I think for a man who loved you with your scars, that emotional part would be even stronger. Are you saying there is someone?"

"There was, but I might have blown it."

"Have you talked to him? Grant and I went to a marriage therapist. You would be surprised how much talking helps."

"I don't know if I am ready to talk."

Candace could hear little voices in the background.

"The kids just got home from school. I need to run. Don't wait too long."

"Bye, sis."

"Bye. I love you."

"Love you too." Candace disconnected the call.

She read the text Colin had sent this morning.

She wasn't ready to talk. A yawn escaped. Having called in sick after a sleepless night, a nap seemed like an excellent idea. She slipped into bed and thought about all the moments she had missed with her sister. Next time she saw the reverend, she would have to thank him.

Hours later, she woke to the ringing of her phone. Mandy.

"Hey, friend. What is going on? Colin is worried, but he isn't talking. Says you aren't answering."

Candace slid out of bed, still in her robe. Her stomach rumbled, protesting its lack of lunch and dinner. "I don't even know where to begin."

"Why don't you try?"

Candace's phone vibrated. Probably a text from Colin. She ignored it. "Last night things got, well, a bit—" *Heavy, embarrassing, and out of hand*? "Let's just say I didn't do a good job of telling Colin it was breast cancer."

Her phone vibrated again. Then again. Candace looked at her phone. It was Zoe.

—911 call, please.

—NOW!

Mandy started to say something, but Candace cut her off. "Zoe is trying to reach me. She says it is an emergency."

Candace hung up and called her cousin. "Zoe, what is wrong?"

"I was attacked, again."

Once again, the universe reminded Candace that there were bigger problems than just her own. As she listened to the story, she wondered if Abbie could get ahold of the plane and arrange a visit to New York so she could help Zoe as well as give herself more time before she had to face Colin.

nineteen

THE SUDDEN TRIP TO NEW York baffled him. Candace had texted late last night.

—I know we need to talk. Give me a couple days. I didn't mean to tell you that way. Family emergency. I need to get to Zoe. Mandy and Abbie are going to work on the premiere. 1 2 3

The numbers baffled him.

According to Daniel, the emergency included Mandy, Abbie, and Harmon's jet. Daniel said he didn't know why, other than there had been an urgent call from Zoe. Since the women had already discussed going out because of the Hearthfire premiere of the movie Sean and Tessa had been extras for, everything quickly fell into place.

Colin hoped the emergency wasn't just Candace trying to get away.

His phone rang.

It was Nick. "Do you have a minute? I need help with a problem."

"You got them too?"

"Not exactly me. Zoe. I need you to legally erase everything you can find on the web, especially social media, for the last two or three years."

Colin opened his laptop. "That is a tall and vague order."

"But you are the only person I know who can do it." Nick's voice was desperate.

"Do I get to know why?" He typed Zoe's name in the search.

"I think you will figure it out soon enough. Can I help you with your problems?"

"Unless you understand women, probably not. I goofed, and Candace isn't talking to me. I think she left town with Mandy. I took the wrong door out of the friend zone." Colin couldn't really describe what had happened last night, so he used vague phrases from some of the articles he'd read over the summer.

"Hey, I finally found my way into the friend zone. Might I suggest you let her give you a black eye?"

"There is a story there. Maybe we can get things to change by the premiere."

"Premiere?" asked Nick,

Rats. As one of Sean's friends, Nick should have been invited. Colin hoped he hadn't said the wrong thing. "The Hearthfire Christmas movie Sean and Tessa were scenery for. Mandy and Candace have been working on plans for weeks now in the old theater in Blue Pines."

"I don't think I got an invite."

"Oh, you will. They haven't sent them yet. I'll just—" Colin paused. A social media post came up, calling Zoe a liar for claiming she'd been assaulted by a fellow student. Comments raged on both sides. Newspaper articles were linked to the post. Zoe wasn't named, but it all fit together. "Oy. That is why Zoe transferred schools her senior year. This guy smeared her in everything from the university paper to the most unpopular social media websites. Why do people have to be such jerks?"

"I wish I knew."

"Give me a couple hours. I can't do much about the newspapers other than trying to boost other things in the rankings in front of them. The papers don't say her name, but with the social media posts, I managed to quickly connect them. If there are court records, I can't touch those, but she still shouldn't be named. Did you know Zoe won a few awards for her design, including one for Wolf Trapp, the National Park, and at the county fair for 4-H things? I'll push those stories to the top in the searches. Anyone specific I need to hide this from?"

"Sleazy lawyers…"

Yikes. Colin didn't ask. Candace's urgent run to New York was more than a cover story. Terrible timing, but probably necessary. "I'll do my best. With any luck, they will only find her detasseling-corn speed record and her prize heifer during a preliminary search and won't look further. A bullying complaint to a couple of the networks should delete some of this permanently. They are too afraid of lawsuits. See you at the premiere."

The call disconnected. Colin waded through the sludge, doing whatever he legally could. He reported some of the posts to the social media companies with a bullying complaint using words like *slander* and *#metoo*. Some of the posts were removed within the hour. Without the posts, the nameless newspaper articles were harder to connect.

He ran a program that would help redirect the popular search engines to innocuous articles and to other women named Zoe Wilson. Short of breaking the law, he couldn't do much else other than set up watches like he had on Mandy's accounts. Zoe hadn't posted much in the past year and a half. Wise woman.

He texted Candace.

I hope all goes well this weekend. Can't wait for you to get back.

He didn't expect an answer anytime soon.

Candace spent the short plane ride sleeping, mostly to avoid talking about her own situation. Everyone was concerned about Zoe and trying to figure out the best way to go see her.

As they landed, Candace got a text from Tessa.

—Zoe is heading to our place.

Thanks. I'll come straight there.

The driver dropped her off at Tessa's first and took Mandy and Abbie to meet with the theater owner.

Zoe ran across the room and hugged Candace. "Why are you here?"

"I heard Sean and Tessa were having a party and thought I would drop by."

Nick stood up from the couch. Candace tried to cover her shock. Her cousin had been sitting next to a man after last night. A man with a black eye.

Before she could ask any questions, Tessa spoke. "Nick's driver is still in the driveway. We need girl time. Since there is chocolate in the house and none at the new one, we claim this as our temporary girls' clubhouse."

Sean kissed his wife before leaving. "I'll take Nick over to see the new carpet. We'll have Sebastian drive us."

Nick stopped in front of Zoe. "Enjoy today and stop worrying about my eye."

As soon as the door closed, Zoe turned to Candace. "What are you really doing here?"

"Last night when I got your 911 text, I was on the phone with Mandy, hence the reason I didn't pick up but called you back when I got the text. After you hung up, I called her back and told her I thought we should all get together now. Abbie got involved, and around six this morning, we headed for the airport. Mandy and Abbie are down at the theater with baby Joy. Your being here saved us coming into town to surprise you. Now, what happened to Nick's eye?"

"He startled me, and after last night, I acted before I thought. I know his eye has got to hurt, but he is too nice to say anything about it. I am not sure what to do." Zoe rung her hands. "He says he believes me about everything that happened two years ago."

Nick was ten times better for her cousin than she could have ever guessed. The jerk who was Zoe's boyfriend two years ago had dumped her shortly after the rape, siding with those who claimed she was only crying wolf. Candace grabbed Zoe's hand. "Tell me everything." Surprisingly, Zoe focused more on Nick's kindness than on the assault by her manager the night before. Thanks to nearly two years of self-defense training, the outcome was much different than the one Zoe had endured on campus.

"Then this morning I blurted out my deepest darkest secret to Nick, and he didn't react like I expected. I've been waiting for him to run away from me all morning. At least he didn't react like some of the guys did back—" Zoe didn't finish the sentence. Every vile post, every letter to the editor, and the joke of a trial ran through Candace's mind. She had been helpless to help Zoe other than to stand by her side. Having witnessed Zoe's near breakdown and subsequent avoidance of men, she never thought there would come a day when her cousin would confide in one.

Candace continued to question Zoe, satisfied that this time her cousin was going to stand strong.

Tessa drew Zoe into a hug. "When you know you can discuss your greatest fears with a man, he is the one you keep forever."

Zoe turned to Candace. "You never said why you were on the phone with Mandy in the first place. What is going on?"

"I told Colin all about my cancer in a moment of temper, and now I can't face him."

"Now it's time for 'Questions with Zoe.' What happened?"

Candace took a deep breath. "For weeks I've been thinking about how to tell him about my falsies, but I kept chickening out, putting it off."

"Being the queen of procrastination?" Zoe shook her head.

"Yes. I didn't want to tell him, because I was his first kiss and he deserves to have a real woman."

Mandy put her arm around Candace's shoulders. "You are a real woman. One with the scars to prove it."

Candace wiped away an annoying tear. "We were kissing, he'd been in Hong Kong, and, well, things got more intense than I usually let them. You know what I mean." Candace waved her hands helplessly. Knowing she was blushing only added to her embarrassment. It didn't help that Mandy, Abbie, and Tessa all smiled knowingly. "Anyway, he was about to discover my prosthetics on his own. I was mad at myself for not telling him and for letting things get that passionate, so I took out my falsies and handed them to him."

"What did he say?" asked Zoe.

"I don't think he said anything. I ran out. People who realize I have had cancer, which is almost everyone who sees my hair two days in a row, always tell me I am so brave, but I'm not. I couldn't face his reaction." Candace buried her head in her hands. Tessa and Abbie hadn't reacted to the news. She wasn't sure if that was good or bad, and she wasn't sure if either had known before.

Zoe wrapped her arms around her and let her cry. "One of the things that got me through the last two years is you telling me life was mostly the choices we make when bad things happen."

Candace looked up. "I don't see where I still have any choices left."

Mandy rocked Joy in the carrier with her foot. "You have a choice to talk to him. I called you yesterday because you were not answering him and he was worried. Colin isn't like Daniel. He doesn't have much experience when it comes to dating. He wouldn't tell me what happened, but he begged me to check on you."

Abbie spoke for the first time. "Maybe it isn't your choice that matters. It could be Colin's. The question for you is can you handle it if he wants a relationship? I don't think you are as afraid of him leaving as you are of him holding on to you until you come to your senses and hold on to him too."

Afraid of him holding on or being held? Ridiculous. Everyone wanted to be held. Even her.

No one spoke for a long time. Across town, the church bells chimed the hour. Tessa stood. "How about we have some of that chocolate?"

twenty

COLIN STUDIED THE SKY FROM his observatory. One of the planes he'd been tracking in the last half hour had to be the Harmon's jet. According to Daniel, Mandy and the baby would be back by dinnertime. He'd been tempted to alter Sabrina's programming so she would tell him if Candace had returned to her apartment. But that was crossing too many lines. Another plane flew by, but it was on its initial climb, not landing.

"Candace Wilson is on the elevator. Should I grant access to the penthouse?"

"Sabrina, yes!" Colin hurried down the spiral staircase and through the rooms. The elevator opened just as he got there. He searched for something to say. Candace held up a shopping bag. He took it. The T-shirt said, "I'm with stupid." Candace moved to his right side so that if he put it on it would point at her.

"I don't get it." Colin put the shirt back in the bag.

"I shouldn't have told you the way I did, and I shouldn't have tried to shut you out. I am stupid."

"I don't think you're stupid." Colin led the way into the more formal sitting room. Candace sat on one end of the couch, and he took the other.

The silence begged to be broken. Candace took a breath. "Shortly after my sixteenth birthday, my mother was diagnosed with stage-four breast cancer. She taught my sister and me how to do self-exams. I found a lump, but cancer in teen girls is rare. We only got it checked because my grandmother had also had breast cancer. Mine was fast moving and had already spread to a couple of lymph nodes. Dad found mom a spot in Houston at MD Anderson, hoping they could do something. I went too. After conferring with several doctors, I decided to remove not only the breast with the tumor but the healthy one, too. Mom and I had our mastectomies the same day. I didn't know it until we were in Indy and I talked to Dad, but she only did it to support me. It didn't change her outcome. Because it had spread to our lymph nodes and to her bones, we both had chemo. Mom and Dad didn't tell Crystal and I how serious Mom's was until it got near the end. When I made the choice to remove the healthy one, it seemed logical since there was a genetic factor. I figured since I only had ten years to live, I would never get married anyway."

"You had already started your ten-year plan?"

"No, just my bucket list. My first thing was a photo with Mom in the Texas bluebonnets. Then I wanted to kiss one man each year until I died. Looking back, that was stupid. I pretty much just kissed anyone. People accuse men of using women. I wasn't any better. It wasn't until Mandy fell for Daniel that I saw my folly. I was on number nine. I never did kiss number ten."

Colin held up his hand. "So I am number ten?"

She grabbed his hand and held it between hers, sending warmth up his arm. "Or you are number one of my new plans."

Number one sounded good. Which reminded him about 1 2 3. What did it mean?

"I'd meant to tell you about the mastectomies since Indy. I knew things were getting serious, and I knew you needed the choice to find someone who was whole. But I couldn't do it. I'd made up my mind to tell you that night, but one thing led to another, and then I was regretting my choice to not leave the healthy one just in case … in case …" Tears formed in her eyes.

Colin pulled out his handkerchief and handed it to her. *I love you Candace. It doesn't matter.*

"Thanks."

Colin cleared his throat and opened his mouth to speak, but Candace held up her hand.

"There is more. One of the more obvious side effects of my treatment is my lack of hair. Permanent hair loss was a known but rare side effect of the new drug they used on me. A more common one was early onset menopause. As in I have been having hot flashes, et cetera, for a year, and I am not even twenty-eight. I can't have children."

The news didn't surprise him. "I wondered if that might be the case. I did a lot of research over the weekend. You have been in remission for a decade, so you have excellent chances of the cancer not reoccurring, especially since you chose to remove healthy tissue. I think I'd rather have you around for fifty years with two scars than the alternative."

"Do you have any idea how ugly they are?" Candace let go of his hand and started to lift the hem of her shirt.

Colin reached out and stopped her tugging the shirt back down. "If you hadn't had the mastectomies, would you show me your chest?"

"Not until the wedding night." Candace blushed. "I mean, I wouldn't show any man until then."

"Then don't show me now. Your scars are a special part of you, showing your strength and courage. They should be saved for a special time."

Candace looked at him in disbelief. "But they are so ugly."

"I am told beauty is largely a part of one's perspective." He leaned closer and removed her wig and the wig cap beneath it. "You are beautiful."

Tears ran down her face.

Colin panicked.

Candace laid a hand on either side of his face. "I love you, Colin McClain Ogilvie." Then she kissed him.

She knew his middle name. She knew him. He kissed her back, hoping she would understand the things he didn't know how to say.

Candace didn't want to leave, but Sabrina and her alarm feature were annoyingly persistent.

"Cinderella needs to leave the ball. Dong, dong…"

Candace lifted her head from Colin's shoulder. They had simply talked for the last hour. "Did you really program her to say that?"

"After our last kissing session started getting more intense, I thought it would be good to have our AI chaperon keep us in check. It was funnier in my mind."

Candace got up and slipped her shoes and wig on. "It is kind of funny."

Colin stood up with her. "How about that ball I promised you? How about Thursday night, since Friday is the Harmon's party?"

"Will Sabrina be there?"

"My mother would kill me if I installed an AI out at the house."

"Will your mother be there?"

"Probably not."

Not too disappointing. The couple of times she had been around Colin and his mother, he was stiff and nervous. "Do I need a ball gown?"

"I think every woman should wear an appropriate gown to her own ball."

"I left all my bridesmaids dresses at Art House."

"Buy a new one."

Candace smiled, knowing he had no clue how much a gown cost. "Nick doesn't pay me that well."

"Then let me buy you one. And don't say no. I've watched all your old roommates get something extravagant. Daniel gave Mandy a house. I am just giving you a dress. Go shopping with Mandy and have her send the bill to me."

Candace kissed him lightly on the cheek. "Yes, my prince. I'll have a new gown by Thursday."

"Cinderella needs to leave the ball. Dong, dong."

Candace hurried to the elevator before the AI tried something more drastic, like an electric shock.

She set her alarm and got ready for bed. After putting her prosthetics in their individual boxes, she looked in the mirror. He thought her scars could be beautiful. She pondered that for a moment. Colin certainly had no problem with her bald head. In a few months, she might believe it. Fortunately, Colin was not one to make quick decisions.

twenty-one

THE RED LAMBORGHINI LOOKED LIKE it had never been driven. Candace snuck a peek at the odometer: 8,942. It hadn't. "THIS WAS THE BEST I could do for a coach. All the pumpkins were tied up for Halloween parties this weekend. My mother even took her limo to a party."

So Mrs. Ogilvie would not be in attendance. The revelation didn't shock Candace. Although Candace suspected they cared about each other, mother and son didn't have a particularly close relationship. His mother had probably never figured out a way to talk to a boy who held conversations with computers. She ran her hand over the supple leather seat. "I think this will do very nicely. I only worry that my green dress looks too Christmassy with the red of the car."

"Well, you look stunning in it. I only wish I had more people to invite to the ball. But at least with Araceli and Kyle we will have four couples."

"I am glad they could come since Tessa and Zoe couldn't."

"I still don't see why they couldn't just fly over for the night."

Candace laughed at his fake pout. Zoe was now publicly dating Nick, who'd managed to have his fair share of paparazzi hounds—not as many as Daniel, but still enough that Zoe's photo had made it into the gossip vlogs this week. "I think they had prior engagements. Not everyone keeps an open social calendar." It was lucky Mandy and Abbie and their husbands were free.

The mansion was a fantastic specimen of turn-of-the-century craftsmanship. Colin parked in the circular drive, and a man wearing what seemed to be British-style livery opened the doors. "Uniforms?"

"Mom likes them for special events. Since we are having a ball, Mandy thought it would add to the theme."

"Does that make me Cinderella?" Even on the magical bucket-list night in the castle, she never felt as much like a princess as she did when the butler opened the door and announced them into the ballroom, where the three other couples waited. Overhead, electric candles twinkled from the chandelier. Where she expected to see some sort of electronic speakers, a quartet played.

As Colin led her to the center of the floor, she looked at Mandy and momentarily dropped her jaw. Her friend got the message and giggled. Colin nodded to the musicians, and they started to play a waltz. Candace let her eyes flutter closed, knowing that Colin's expert leading would do all the work. She felt like a princess in his arms. When the tempo changed, she opened her eyes to find Colin studying her.

"I don't know that I have ever danced with a woman who closed her eyes before."

"I just wanted to just feel everything for a moment. But it looks amazing, too."

The other couples joined them. Colin twirled her in the direction of the terrace. What would a ballroom be without a terrace for lovers to sneak away to?

The cool air teased at her, and she leaned into Colin for warmth and the promised kiss.

Colin led her to a bench in the corner. "I didn't plan this very well. In my mind it was warmer." He knelt in front of her, and her heart began to race. No, not yet.

"Candace Lucy Wilson, will you dance waltzes with me all the days of your life?"

The diamond glistened in the light that poured out the door to the ballroom. She tried to speak. *No* was the wrong answer. *Yes* was impossible. Wasn't it? She tried to force the acceptance out, but it was caught in a grip of fear.

Colin waited, the furrow in his brow deepening.

She tried to breathe and couldn't.

His shoulders slumped. He mumbled something, and his face faded as darkness overcame her.

Colin caught her just as she tumbled off the bench.

"Daniel!"

Colin's yell brought not only Daniel but the other couples and some of the staff.

Mandy reached his side first. "Did she faint?"

"I don't know. I've never seen anyone faint before."

"What were you doing out here?" Daniel took off his coat and placed it over Candace.

"Proposing?" Colin answered as quietly as he could, but it was evident from the gasps that everyone had heard him.

"I think she is coming around. Let's get her inside," said Abbie.

Daniel helped him stand. Candace was lighter than he thought she would be.

Araceli took the pillows off a nearby davenport. As Colin set Candace down, she moaned.

"Everyone step back to give her some air." Abbie's bodyguard personality came out as she ushered everyone back.

Colin turned to the other men. "Your wives didn't faint, did they?"

Preston covered his mouth with his hand, but his eyes still held laughter. "I've proposed several times and never seen that reaction. Although I did have one end up in a fountain screaming."

Colin kept one eye on Candace. Mandy handed her a glass of water. He couldn't hear what the woman was saying.

Abbie came over. "I'll take Candace home. She is still feeling a little shaky. Colin, she said she would talk to you soon."

The women left.

"Well, guys, I guess the ball is over." Colin searched for something he could offer them. But even his mother's etiquette drills didn't help. His brain refused to process anything. He wanted to be alone, afraid one of his friends would discover the source of Candace's distress. He couldn't face the humiliation. "Perhaps you should see to your wives?"

"Whose car did they take?" asked Kyle. "Did they take a driver or a bodyguard?"

Daniel and Preston laughed at the same time. "Abbie."

Kyle shook his head. "I hardly ever think of her that way."

"Well, it looks like I need a ride. Daniel?" Preston asked.

Within minutes, Colin was alone with a dozen staff members.

He trudged up to his old bedroom and tried to figure out what he'd done wrong.

Candace woke up with the biggest headache of her life. She wandered out to the kitchen in search of an ice pack. Advice—she needed some. She went back into the bedroom and found her phone.

She dialed Reverend Cavanagh's number, but it went straight to voicemail.

She scrolled down and hit the icon for Dad.

"Morning, sweetie."

"Dad can I come visit for the weekend?"

"Sure, why?"

"I'll explain when I get there."

Candace hung up and called in sick again. At this rate, Nick was going to fire her.

The ice wasn't touching her headache, so she dug through her essential oils until she found a blend she'd had success with in the past.

Tossing a pair of jeans and a couple of shirts into a bag, she headed out. At the door, she whispered, "Sabrina, don't tell him," just in case the AI was watching her apartment, too.

All weekend, Colin waited for Candace to return his calls or texts, but a reply never came. Her car wasn't in the garage, and according to security, she'd left early Saturday morning. Her disappearance could have had something to do with the fact that Zoe and Nick were all over the news. Even if it wasn't really them. No doubt Candace was somewhere dealing with the fallout. Colin had been so busy yesterday preparing for his proposal that he had missed the media circus wrongly accusing his friend of assault and dredging up Zoe's past.

Even if he had seen it, there was little he could have done to help.

He hoped Candace was with Zoe. The other alternative was that she'd run from him after his proposal.

Late Sunday afternoon, Colin texted Nick.

Sorry I couldn't bury Zoe's life deeper.

—Not your fault.

Is she talking to you?

—She left me a goodbye note.

Colin wasn't sure how to respond to that.

I'm not sure if the carousel will be finished anytime soon. The artist may or may not have quit.

—Candace? Why?

I proposed. I thought she would be willing after she came back from Blue Pines. I guess I don't understand women. Colin typed the understatement of the year.

—**You and me both, my friend.**

I was serious when I said it is easier to hack the Pentagon than it is to understand a woman.

—**My guess is it is easier to hack North Korea's military servers.**

Nah. Only took me two hours. Just kidding. Haven't tried that one.

—-**I'm relieved to know that. Don't.**

Not that desperate. I still have Mandy, the secret weapon. She's calling. Bye.

"Hi, Mandy."

"Hey, how are you holding up?"

"Fine. Please tell me you've heard from her." Any little clue, please.

"She went to her dad's. She says she will meet us in Blue Pines."

"She is taking the week off?" He rubbed his forehead. Day 564 wasn't supposed to be like this. It was supposed to be a countdown to day one of the rest of their lives.

"Sorry, Colin."

"Do you think it's a no?"

"She didn't say no, which probably means she is working through things. I know fainting isn't the best response, but she has a lot going on right now. Since she didn't respond, there is still a chance she will say yes. Sorry."

Colin hung up. He wanted to know more, to hear how she was in her own voice.

An hour later, he got a text from her.

Please come to Blue Pines. Premiere—November 2. I am visiting Dad.

—**I'll be there.**

Thanks. 1 2 3

Maybe all was not lost. He went in search of Janie and found her in the kitchen. "What does it mean when a girl tells you one, two, three?"

She stopped stirring the pot on the stove in front of her. "I don't know all of your young-people lingo. But when I counted at my children, it was never a good thing."

The housekeeper could have added or counted at him. How many cookies had he lost over the years for not listening the first time?

There had to be another answer. Colin retreated to his office. "Sabrina, what could one, two, three mean?"

twenty-two

CANDACE CHECKED THE SLIDESHOW SHE'D made again—well, her father had made, after she nearly sent her laptop through the window. She tried writing a love note first and decided that notes like hers were better off hidden in hollow swans than ever read. Hopefully this would convey the thoughts in her heart better than words on paper.

The week had been cathartic. Crystal had come down, and they'd had three days of crying and laughing, watching old videos, including one she had never seen. Mom had left a video letter to her. Candace wondered when her mother had found time to record it without her knowing.

Candace brought it up again and played her favorite part.

"I looked in your notebook last night. I know that makes me a terrible mom, snooping in your journal or life plan. But by the time you know about it, well, I won't be around to yell at. I want you to throw that book away. I am not sure where you got the idea you had ten years to live. But you are wrong. No doctor ever said that about you. I wonder if you heard Dr. Kay discussing that old car of his. Anyway, please throw it away and plan to live, laugh, and love. Though I didn't get to grow old with your father or see my grandbabies, I don't regret a day of my life with you."

"Please make a new plan for life …"

Candace turned it off.

She had a plan.

Reverend Cavanagh said he would pray for her and her plan. Before she left for the airport, she said one more little prayer.

Colin joined the others gathered in the private dining room of O'Malley's for the pre-show party. He looked around the table at Daniel and Mandy, Tessa and Sean, Araceli and Kyle, and Abbie and Preston. Zoe sat next to Nick. Colin needed to ask Nick about that. The only empty seat was next to—Candace got up from her chair and came over to him. She reached up and pulled him down into a kiss.

All thought fled.

Gradually he became aware of clapping. Candace ended the kiss.

"Knock it off, you guys. You are making Colin blush," Candace scolded their friends.

Colin didn't care if he died of blushing as long as it was because he was in Candace's arms.

"Come sit down, you two. You can do more of that later." Tessa waved them over to the table.

The rest of the dinner seemed an eternity as Colin wondered when later would come.

As the closing credits of the Hearthfire Christmas movie that captured Tessa and Sean's first kiss started to roll, Candace took a deep breath. In fifteen minutes, the room would empty and her encore show would play. Araceli started toward the side of the stage to make the announcement encouraging the majority of the audience to cross the street to the community center for refreshments. At the other end of the room, someone yelled, "Hey! Nick Gooding is engaged!"

Candace whipped around to see her cousin kissing Nick Gooding.

Kissing.

In public.

Engaged.

When?

She looked at each of her friends. One after the other shrugged as they clapped and cheered. Only Colin smiled. He had known!

Colin leaned over so only Candace could hear him. "That isn't how they planned to tell us."

"How do you know?"

"Nick asked me to keep everyone here when the crowd left."

"Oh."

Zoe worked her way down the row, gathering hugs from the roommates. When she reached Candace, they stared at each other for a moment.

Candace pulled her into a hug. "Why didn't you tell me?"

"I didn't have a chance to tell you. We wanted to tell my parents first."

"And they were on the cruise." Candace finished the sentence.

"We finally reached them on the way over."

They hugged again.

Araceli took the stage and tapped the mike. "Ladies and gentlemen, Hearthfire and Blue Pines friends, we invite you to have refreshments at the community center, where you can mix and mingle. Locals, if you don't have tickets for your families and friends for tomorrow's shows yet, they will be available at the center."

A few people gathered their coats, but most just stood around talking.

Araceli recaptured the mike. "Did I mention they are Mrs. Clark's sugar cookies? Three-time winner of the Blue Pines Christmas bake-off? First come, first serve! Go eat!"

The room started to clear. Colin tried to leave.

Candace held on to his hand. "Stay for a minute."

Soon only their row and a few security guards remained.

Araceli retook the stage. "It is the first Friday of November, and I hereby call the last meeting of the Friday Night Art Society to order. We are all going our separate ways and starting new projects and new lives. As the unofficial secretary, I have a few items of business, but first a word from Candace, our mentor, friend, and landlord."

Candace's legs shook as she took the mike from Araceli. "Lights, please." She waited as the house lights dimmed and the video she'd made began to play.

"Ten years ago, I made a ten-year plan." The spiral-bound notebook came up on the screen, the pages turning as she spoke. "I made a bucket list and started checking off each item." Photos of Candace in various places around the country slid across the screen. "I made some goals, and broke some, like the time I tried being a vegan and decided life was too short to live without ice cream or bacon. Or even bacon ice cream. But this July, I reached the end of my ten-year plan and found myself at a different place than I'd planned." The last page of the notebook turned, revealing a sketch of a tree stretching over a headstone, a butterfly lifting off toward the sun. "At my annual cancer check, my doctor told me it was time to make a new plan, not a ten-year plan but a fifty-year plan." A blank page showed on the screen. Candace's hand appeared with a pencil in it. She started drawing on a blank piece of paper. "I struggled to come up with a plan." On the screen, her hands ripped the paper and started on a new one. "My cousin Zoe was the first to say out loud what my plan should be. Now I know what my plan is." The drawing moved in high speed. "In fifty years, I want to be surrounded by you, my friends, as I celebrate my fiftieth wedding anniversary."

The lights came up. Candace took a deep breath, then whispered one last prayer. *Please.*

"Colin Ogilvie. You asked me a question a couple weeks ago. Now it is my turn. Will you start the new year as my husband?" There it was. She no longer had any secrets from her friends. Opening up to her father and sister had given her the confidence to share with her friends. These people were like family to her. She had reached the corner and was turned in a new direction. *Please don't be a dead end*!

Colin ran up to the stage and grabbed her around the waist. "Are you sure?"

"Positive." Candace stood on her toes and wrapped her arms around his neck. Her lips met his twice before she settled in for a deeper kiss to the cheering of their friends. The mike slipped from her fingers and bounced loudly on the stage.

Colin dipped her and broke the kiss. "One, two, three. I love you too."

"I knew you would figure that out."

"Actually, Sabrina did. I think I finally have the glitches fixed."

Somewhere in the background, her friends were still cheering, but Candace ignored them and wondered how hard it would be to program Sabrina to lock them in after the wedding.

epilogue

Five years later on an Indiana airstrip near the Art House.
Colin greeted Candace with a kiss at the door to their new plane. As she boarded, she asked him where their kids were.

"My mother wanted to spoil them for a few days, and I decided I would spoil you." Once Colin had guided her to one of the plush seats at the center of the plane, the copilot closed the door, then signaled for them to buckle up before he joined the pilot in the cockpit.

"They tire you out after only three days?" Seven-year-old Porter and his biological siblings—five-year-old Pollyanna and three-year-old Peter—had been with Colin and Candace for the nearly eighteen months since their widowed mother had lost her battle with breast cancer and the couple had adopted them.

"No, they did not." Colin looked slightly offended. "It was Abbie and Preston's triplets who did. Mathematically it should be impossible for three four-year-olds to cause so much chaos. Somehow they'd conned most of the other children into joining them, including Peter. None of us were too upset to break up the party when we got Mandy's call. Poor Polly received more than enough teasing and was more than willing to go to Grandma's for a visit, which apparently includes Disneyland. Although I think she might have been just as happy to go to the corner park as long as the triplets were not there."

"So Mandy going into labor early was a blessing?" Candace braced for takeoff.

"Better now than during the ribbon cutting in two weeks." The dream of an indoor amusement park for terminally ill children had taken the financial backing of all six families to complete. The invention of a bacteria-resistant polymer coating had allowed the old merry-go-round to be a central feature. Housed an hour west of Dallas in a multibuilding complex connected by tunnels, "Robyn's Place" boasted not only a fun family escape but a fully staffed children's medical facility hidden in a castle. Children who had been cleared by their physicians could stay up to one week at no cost, along with their immediate family. The dedication had been set for the day that would have been Robyn Wilson's fifty-fifth birthday.

"It was definitely better that she cut the last meeting of the Friday Night Art Society short than miss the ribbon cutting. Kudos to you for your app working so well." Candace took off her wig.

Colin kissed her before answering. "Daniel was glad to get her to South Bend for the delivery. The county hospital isn't equipped to handle premature births. By the way, the doctor thinks they will be able to release little Mae from the NICU in less than two weeks."

"I know. Mandy video chatted with me this morning. Other than being born six weeks early and being small, there are not any major complications."

As the plane lifted above the intermittent clouds. Colin rubbed the back of Candace's hand. "So, how was your week with the girls?"

"Let me show you. We made a video." Candace pulled out her tablet and pushed play.

The former members of the Friday Night Art Society sat around their old painted kitchen table turning the pages of the photo books Zoe had designed.

"I love this shot. How did you manage to get it, Abbie?" Araceli pointed to Candace catching Zoe's bouquet at her day-before-Christmas-Eve wedding.

Abbie turned to the same page in her book. "That was easy. We all knew Zoe would continue with tradition and aim it at Candace. So I focused my camera on Candace and waited."

"Who caught Candace's bouquet?" Tessa turned to the pages showing the New Year's Eve wedding.

Mandy balanced her book on her rounded middle. "Daniel's old secretary, Bonnie. She ended up marrying Daniel's old lawyer, Morgan. They are the best stand-in grandparents. Joy and little Danny love them to death. Bonnie has already knitted this one her first blanket." Mandy rubbed her bulging belly and made a face.

"Please tell me that is not a contraction." Abbie half rose from her seat.

"No. Just a kick that makes me question this little one's future. I am only thirty-two weeks."

Abbie sat back down. "Well, you happen to have the worst timing when it comes to deliveries. First my wedding reception, then during the dedication of Candace's teen cancer wing of the hospital. Forgive me if I am suspicious since this is the first day of our weeklong reunion."

"Don't worry. Mandy is testing out Colin's new contraction app. If her body even hints at a Braxton-Hicks, there will be an ambulance at the door. You know Daniel. Besides, Nick, Daniel, and Colin are doing a ribbon cutting in three weeks at Robyn's Place. If Mandy is going to disrupt anything, it will be the dedication since it will have national news coverage." Candace flipped through the pages of her book.

"I have no intention of going into labor during the ceremony. I want the story to be about the children and the carousel that started all of this, not about me. Besides, Zoe is closer to her due date."

Zoe groaned and stirred her ginger ale with a straw. "And I wish I was even closer. Nearly four years and a gazillion doctor visits so I could have morning sickness for seven months straight."

Candace sighed as she watched the video of Zoe. Her cousin hadn't shared much about her trial with infertility and multiple miscarriages. Candace wished Zoe had shared more as Candace had long-ago accepted the impossibility of having her own children. Zoe's pain and grief were the catalysts for Candace's decision to adopt.

Candace rapped on the table. "I have an item of business. I have been trying to decide what to do with the Art House for some time now. With my children, I don't make it down here as often as I would like to. I am torn about selling the place as who else would appreciate all the Friday and Saturday nights we spent decorating? Araceli has proposed it become a scholarship house for some of her Haitian children. But before I donate it, I wanted everyone's thoughts."

Tessa stood and went to the stained-glass window above the sink. "This was one of my first windows. I named it Morning Blessing because of the way the sunrise would light it up. I think I like the idea that it could bless future generations of students. I'll be honest—I hoped my own daughters would want to come here someday, but they are going to find their own path, just like we did."

Abbie's phone rang. She shook her head. "It looks like the kids stole Preston's phone again. I'll be back in a minute." She exited the room.

Abbie rejoined them. "Crisis solved. Don't worry. The father and kids' movie night is back on track, and none of your children were in any danger."

The women laughed.

The video ended with a close-up of the quote wall in the laundry room.

Don't let fences keep friends out. —Mandy

Broken glass doesn't equal broken dreams. —Tessa

When added to the ugliest of walls, beauty brings a bounty of blessings. —Araceli

Embrace the unexpected in life, and it will bring you joy. —Abbie

When you meet one of the good guys, close your eyes and trust. That is the key. —Zoe

Never put limits on yourself that God hasn't given you. —Candace

Candace blinked back the tears. Colin's arms came around her. "Why are you crying?" He handed her a handkerchief.

"I am just sad it's over."

Colin shook his head. "It isn't. You still have forty-five years to go. It's in your fifty-year plan, remember?"

"How can I forget?" The sketch she'd used as one of the final slides of her proposal now hung in her studio. Candace leaned into Colin's chest and watched the clouds float by the window. Or was the plane floating by the clouds?

The End

acknowledgments

WHEN I STARTED WRITING MENDING Fences I never thought that it would lead to another book or five. I have had so much fun researching an imaginary world beyond my own.

TAMMY AND NANETTE ARE SO willing to help make all my projects better and to read things so many times even in late night texts. I would never make it through a day without Sally and Cindy whose advice keeps me going. Thank you wonderful ladies.

Thanks also to Michele at Eschler Editing for her edits and finding oh so many little things to fix; any mistakes left in this book are not her fault. Nor are my excellent proofreaders to be blamed. Thank you ladies and gents!

My family, for sharing their home with the fictional characters who often got fed better than they did. And my husband who encourages me every crazy step of the way and puts up with all my messy spreadsheets.

And to my Father in Heaven for putting these wonderful people, and any I may have forgotten to mention, in my life. I am grateful for every experience and blessing I have been granted.

about the author

LORIN GRACE WAS BORN IN Colorado and has been moving around the country ever since, living in eight states and several imaginary worlds. She graduated from Brigham Young University with a degree in Graphic Design.

Currently she lives in northern Utah with her husband, four children, and a dog who is insanely jealous of her laptop. When not writing, Lorin enjoys creating graphics, visiting historical sites, museums, and reading.

LORIN IS AN ACTIVE MEMBER of the League of Utah Writers and was awarded Honorable Mention in their 2016 creative writing contest short romance story category. Her debut novel, *Waking Lucy,* was awarded a 2017 Recommended Read award in the LUW Published book contest. In 2018 the first book in this series, Mending Fences with the Billionaire, also received a Recommended Read award.

You can learn more about her, and sign up for her writers club at loringrace.com or at Facebook: LorinGraceWriter

www.ingramcontent.com/pod-product-compliance
Lightning Source LLC
Chambersburg PA
CBHW060420260626
47161CB00005B/1711